Felicia Alexandra is from Ohio. She went to Case Western Resesrve University where she studied pre-med. She has two cats, Leo and Kitty. She is an Aries and likes astrology. Her hobbies are singing, acting and modeling. She once modeled for a race car show and was in the movie unspeakable. She likes listening to pop and rock music and watching scary movies.

This is a work of fiction. Names, characters, businesses, places, events, locales, and incidents are either the products of the author's imagination or used in a fictitious manner. Any resemblance to actual persons, living or dead, or actual events is purely coincidental.

Ordering Information
Quantity sales: Special discounts are available on quantity purchases by corporations, associations, and others. For details, contact the publisher at the address below.

Publisher's Cataloging-in-Publication data
Alexandra, Felicia
Never Been Kissed

ISBN 9798895439302 (Paperback)
ISBN 9798895439319 (ePub e-book)

Library of Congress Control Number: 2025907031

www.austinmacauley.com/us

First Published 2025
Austin Macauley Publishers LLC
40 Wall Street, 33rd Floor, Suite 3302
New York, NY 10005
USA

mail-usa@austinmacauley.com
+1 (646) 5125767

Felicia Alexandra

NEVER BEEN KISSED

AUSTIN MACAULEY PUBLISHERS
LONDON * CAMBRIDGE * NEW YORK * SHARJAH

Chapter 1

And the funny thing about it is, if I had to do it again, I wouldn't have had it any other way.

I don't want to be labeled
I don't want to be mass-produced
I just want to be happy
and if it weren't so damn expensive
I still would probably not take a drop of it

relationships are simple at first
then you fall in love
and the world ends
right on schedule
If you liked me so much
I can't help but wonder
why didn't you come looking for me
I love you but I don't think I could stand being with you
You're just a little too annoying

The world was small and I was even smaller. I think I knew that when I met him. He was everything and anything I ever wanted in life. That's why my heart chased him so hard and was so relieved when it was over. Even so, I know he'll carry a piece of me in his soul for all eternity, just like I do with him. He taught me love was good and real and right and not just a figment of my brilliant imagination. Every day with him was exciting. His presence gave me vertigo. His words made me smart. His love made me strong. But that was a long time ago now. It was thanks to him that I was able to get married to my soulmate and have two beautiful children with my husband. And thanks to him, I regret nothing and fear is a basic sick I'm no longer able to catch.

I wasn't the type of girl to believe in love. Love was for the poets and dancers of the world. I was more like a steam engine running out of steam. I don't know why I'm like this. I used to blame my father because he was a raging alcoholic but when I got older, I realized I could drink more than he could, which was funny to me later. I work. A lot. and that was my prestige. I work for a counseling company that offers advice to the depressed and lonely and I enjoy my work. I lived just on the border of New York City in a quaint apartment that I paid way too much for. I have medium brown hair and brown eyes and I'm twenty-nine and have never been kissed.

I met Sam late one night at a bar I frequented after work. Normally the bar was all regulars so it was strange to me that there would be a new face in the place. He was ridiculously handsome with brown hair and broad shoulders. I stared at him as if he were a computer screen. When he looked back at me I realized what I was doing and turned my stare to my drink in hand. I want to say I was embarrassed he had noticed me but I was secretly happy he had. He approached me moments later and sat down beside me.

"And what is it you're drinking," he asked me. His voice was low and soothing. I was surprised he was even talking to me. The last time that happened to me it was a police officer writing me a DUI. The chair I sat on felt hard and I felt fat and ugly.

"Just straight-up whisky," I replied, finally, feeling shy for possibly the first time in my entire life.

He motioned toward the bartender. "Another drink for the lady. On me," he said. "And your name, if you don't mind me asking."

"Christina Bell," I replied. I couldn't believe it. Was he hitting on me? No one had ever hit on me in my entire life. Was this normal? I wasn't sure the answer to that. All I knew was that I was starting to notice everything in the room. The wooden stools, the booth tables with duct tape holding the seats together, the pictures of beer and women on the walls.

"Sam Fare," he said, shaking my hand. "A pleasure to meet you." A pleasure he called it. Talk about being in the right place at the right time. Maybe her time had come and it was finally her turn to find her soulmate.

I watched him carefully as he talked. His eyes blinded me so it was hard to see his face. He was so attractive in fact that I ended up staring at his left ear for stability. "Ditto," I said, trying to keep up. I was curious to see where this was going.

"And you come here often?" Yes. Which made her wonder why she had never seen him before. Was he new in town? Bored? Experimenting?

The conversation was still going so I figured I must be doing something right. "Only every day," I joked. Phew. Was it just me or was it getting hot in here?

"I feel like I might have met you before," he continued.

"I don't think so." I racked my brain trying to think of a day or night she would've seen him before but she couldn't. He must've mistaken her for someone else. Was that the only reason he was talking to her? Did he think she was someone he had met before?

"Are you sure?" he asked, looking back at me with intense gray eyes.

"I would've remembered." I sighed. Yeah. He definitely had thought she was someone else. That had to be it. "I look like a lot of people," I added. "Keeps me young."

"I suppose." He continued. "You're very pretty. Do you get that a lot?"

I was short and skinny with black hair and blue eyes. I never considered myself attractive. My face was pretty average in my opinion. I wasn't used to the compliment but it gave me a small amount of confidence to talk to him. "Not really," I admitted.

"How old are you?" he asked.

"Twenty-nine," I told him. "And you?"

"Thirty-one."

I couldn't help but wonder why he was asking me so many questions. He paused and I held my breath. I was enjoying the conversation but why was he here? What did he want? Because if it was sex, he could forget. I was a virgin and I didn't plan on losing it tonight, no matter how devastatingly hot this guy was. The idea was much too random for me.

I politely took the drink he bought for me and the remainder of my own drink and downed them quickly. Then I turned to look at him and threw up in his lap. I didn't know what to do. I panicked. I don't think I have ever felt that humiliated before in my entire life. I grabbed a napkin off the counter. "I… I'm sorry," I stammered. "I didn't mean to do that."

"I'll be back," he said. "I'm going to rinse off in the restroom." He got up and left, leaving me alone with my embarrassment.

So much for that. Whether he was hitting on her or not, it didn't really matter now because she had ruined it, like she ruined everything in her life. I grabbed my coat and purse and was just about to run away when he returned, soaked pants as if he had wet himself.

"Are you leaving," he asked.

"Yes. I'm sorry about that. I hope you're not mad. As a matter of fact, I can give you money for a new pair of pants. Would that make it up to you?" I was bumbling and extremely unsure of myself.

"Can I just have your cell phone number?" He asked. "Before you head out."

Really? I was shocked. He wanted my number. This was all so new to me that I didn't know what to say to him. I wanted to leave without giving him my number and get away from him and I didn't want to make a big deal about it but it had been nearly two minutes since she had met Mr. Sam and she was already unable to say no to him. "Sure." She grabbed a napkin and wrote it down for him.

"Here."

He took it. "Thanks. I didn't mean to be in the way of you and your vomit." He joked.

I smiled awkwardly at the joke. "Cute." I put my coat on and swung my purse over my shoulder before heading out. I got to my parked car and climbed inside. It had started to rain, which would normally bother me because I hate rain and driving in it, but I was so embarrassed about my encounter with Mr. Sam that I kind of didn't care right now. The bar was only a couple blocks from my place so it didn't take long to get home. I got out of my Ford Hybrid and got into my apartment. My apartment is very lavender because I like the color purple so I pass violet furniture to my bedroom of purple blankets over a made-up bed.

I stare into the mirror on my vanity. Was I attractive? I put both of my two hands on either side of my face and turned my head from side to side. Mr. Sam had been so strangely interested in her. It confused me. Why did he want to talk to her anyway? They probably had nothing in common. I couldn't think.

Sighing, I went into my bathroom and brushed my teeth before heading to bed. Whatever the reason for his friendliness, she figured she might as well just write it off as her version of a magical one-night stand. Because really, that's probably what that was.

Chapter 2

What would you say
If I said too much
What about too little
I think the words only matter
Because we took the time to articulate them
When I said I love you
Why did you do everything in your power to leave me

So I'm a bit of a perfectionist. That is what they still call that isn't it? Or has that word been gobbled down and defeated by the label obsessive-compulsive disorder? Come on. I'm a therapist. I should know this. Well anyway, I like what I like and I throw out what I don't and if that's not a philosophy of life right there in one sentence, nothing is.

I woke up the next morning to my phone ringing. I was hungover so I almost didn't check to see who it was. I checked anyway. It was Mr. Sam. I picked it up. "Hello?" I mumbled.

"Hey Christina, I thought I'd call and check up with you. I was worried about you. You get home okay?"

"Yeah fine," I stammered. She couldn't believe he had called her. It was a pleasant surprise. She sat up in bed and stifled a yawn. She wondered what he wanted.

"Can I come over?" he asked, completely out of nowhere. Really? Why did he want to come over? They had just met and she wasn't used to bringing strangers back to her house. It felt dangerous. "What was that?" I ended up asking.

"Can I cover over," he said again. He sounded cheerful.

I blinked. Huh? Maybe I heard him right. Maybe I heard him wrong. I didn't know for sure. It was early after all and I was still feeling sick from the night before.

"Can I stop by your place? I have coffee. And aspirin if you need it." He continued as if they had known each other for years. He had such a causal personality. It was hard to not like him. A casual way about himself. Yes, that was the perfect way to describe him.

"No." I blurted out. I was a little intimidated by him. I stopped myself. "I mean, we just met. I'm not used to inviting strangers into my house."

"Fine. Meet me at my house then," he pressed.

"No. Sam. that's the same thing." What was she talking about? What was he talking about? She was starting to get suspicious. We barely knew each other and already he wanted to go somewhere private. And to do what? She was afraid she knew. This man wanted to have sex with her and she wouldn't have it. He was a man. Like all men, he was going to try to get with her and then never call again. No, thank you.

"Tony's Coffee Shop then. Right now."

Was he still talking? She had him figured out. He could drop the innocent act. "I can't. I have to go to work." I replied lamely. Well, it was the truth. As a matter of fact, she was going to be late if she stayed on the phone for too long. "I have to get ready," I finished.

He paused and there was a moment of silence before he pushed, "That's fine. Just call off work for the day. Spend it with me."

She had hit the head on the nail. This guy desperately wanted to get into her pants. "No. Sam. I can't. I really can't. I mean that would be crazy." Even if she wanted to see him again, just a little bit. She couldn't miss work for a one-night stand. She didn't care how charismatic he was.

"Please."

Great not the please thing. He was going to beg nicely and I was going to give him what he wanted. Wasn't that how that worked? Was this a game he played often? Because if he did, he was doing a good job.

I want to think of myself as an independent woman but this guy was breaking down her walls. She had protected her heart for so long to keep anyone from breaking it. Was Mr. Sam here to break her heart? How could she know? Boys are poison when they want something. He wanted her for now, yes maybe for now, maybe even for a day or two or week. But he was dangerous and he was going to end up ruining her if she trusted him.

"Please?" he said again.

So, I don't know if it's the way he said it or my guilty conscious for ruining his pants the night before but just like at the bar, I already felt bad saying no to him. His desperate attempt for attention had worked. She sighed audibly. Meeting at a public place couldn't be that dangerous. She might even survive the sex thing she had avoided her entire life. "Fine."

"Fine, what?" He was toying with her. She just knew it. He was going to do everything right, bring her up onto a pedestal and then he was going to drop her. Why did she do these things to herself? Why did she put herself in these ridiculous scenarios?

Anyway, being the idiot that I am, I agreed to meet with him. Maybe her luck would change and something meaningful could come from it. "I'll meet you at Tony's coffee shop. Just give me a half hour to shower and get dressed." I said finally.

"Cool. I'll meet you in a bit. See you there." He hung up and left me in pure silence.

I yawned and covered my mouth with my hand. I was so tired still. What the hell was wrong with this guy anyway? And what was worse. What was wrong with her for agreeing to meet with him? Was she really going to call off from work? Had she gone crazy?

Only one way to find out she told herself. This might even turn out to be a good thing. She'd never know until she tried. She took a breath. Time to call off work for the day.

She dialed her manager's phone number and told him she wouldn't be able to make it to work today because she was sick. He didn't seem to care as much as I thought he would so that helped my guilty conscious clear up.

When she was done on the phone she went into the bathroom. She'd already done the unthinkable and called off of work for a guy she barely knew. She might as well go all the way with it. I took a shower and dressed in simple jeans and a T-shirt. Her jeans were tighter than she would've liked and she was scared she may have gained weight since the last time she wore them. Deciding not to worry about it, she headed out of her apartment building. The sun was high and bright in the morning sky. I drove to the coffee shop which was about a half-hour drive thinking I was being reckless. I don't know what compelled me to go to him but I think I liked him a little.

You know, sometimes the things we do the most aren't the things we do better and for me, this wasn't what I did the most or anything better. Calling off work had been almost freeing, especially because it was to meet up with a boy I liked. Because I did. I liked him already. Like love at first sight or something. She wasn't sure. Maybe I was just desperate.

I arrived at the shop finding Mr. Sam at a table already, sunglasses covering his pretty eyes. I ordered a small coffee with cream and sat next to him with it. "What's with the sunglasses?"

"Nothing. Just avoiding the cops. They're after me."

I jumped a little in my seat in surprise. "Excuse me?"

"Just kidding. I'm actually a secret agent."

"Another joke."

"You caught me," he chuckled, taking off the sunglasses.

They hadn't talked very much yet so she found it interesting to find out that he was a joker.... And maybe a bit of a jerk. Interesting personality combination. As a therapist, I probably would've written off as a narcissist which was pretty funny in itself. But his laid-back energy did have some benefit to it. She felt more comfortable around him, seeing that he didn't seem to take much very seriously.

"I think I'm starting to understand you," I murmured. She felt shy again like at the bar. What an interesting way to start her day. She was reluctantly enjoying herself.

"I doubt it. No one understands me." He said.

She knew the feeling. When she was little she would constantly feel as if no one really knew her. They might talk to her for a few minutes. Maybe even have lunch together. But did they actually know her? Not really.

"How old are you again?" I asked.

"Thirty-one," he replied.

"I see." What an immature 30-something-year-old. What was he talking about? Or better yet, what was she talking about? I didn't know what else to say so I decided to change the subject. "So you come here a lot?" I asked.

"Only on days, my wife is at work."

"You're married?" Wait he wasn't single. She felt her heart drop in her chest. Great. Just great. And to think she had almost completely lost her mind and thought he might like her, even just a little. So that made these new feelings in her heart unrequited. Sucks.

He smiled at me. “No. Just joking again. Can’t you tell?”

“Not really.” I sighed. Oh, another joke. That must mean he was single. That came as something of a relief to me. I don’t know why I cared so much but I did and aside from his joking, I wanted to know more about him. Even so, to be honest, He was wearing me out already and I had just gotten there. But you know what, I liked it. Sometimes it just fits. Like puzzle pieces. Maybe that was what Mr. Sam was, a puzzle. One to be decoded and appreciated once done so.

“You look beautiful,” he said, putting his sunglasses back on. “But you probably get that a lot?”

Why was he flattering her so much? I was beyond confused and becoming suspicious. Was he playing a joke on her right now? “Not as much as you would think.” I frowned. “What do you want from me anyway? I’m not much of a dater.”

“Who said anything about dating?”

I was taken slightly aback by his words. The walls around her heart were building up again. So maybe he wasn’t married but he definitely wasn’t interested in me in a romantic way. Great. Just when I was starting to get attached. Love was such a pain in the ass, wasn’t it? “Oh. I just thought. I mean. You asked me to come out and meet you. I suppose…” I couldn’t stop stammering. What was I talking about? She thought about leaving but Mr. Sam spoke up, interrupting her thought process.

“You thought this was a date.”

“You know what,” I sighed. “Just never mind.” Forget it. Like he cared what she thought.

“Honey I’m a genie and you’re the princess. If you want this to magically turn into a date then bam. Here it is. It’s a date now.”

Could he get any more obnoxious? He was crazy if he thought she’d stick around after this. I wanted to get to know him better but the more I got to know him, the more cold I realized he was. Like his gray eyes that pierced mine when he looked at me. He was an ice puzzle, one that had to be solved quickly or it would melt.

“I shouldn’t have come here,” I muttered finally. “I shouldn’t have called off work?”

He laughed loudly as if he couldn't stop. This guy didn't like me like that. And she was pretty sure she didn't like him like that either. The only thing she could do now was run away.

"Don't be like that, Babe. I don't bite."

Now I was getting annoyed. Why did he even invite me out if he was just going to reject her? This was typical. She should've known nothing good was going to come out of this. "Well, I do. So I'll see you around."

"You won't stay?" The pure epitome of innocence. He had no idea, did he? How much he had frustrated me already. I picked up my purse and slung the strap over my shoulder. What a waste of time.

"No. I'm going to go back to work and finish my shift." I replied with a huff. It wasn't too late, was it? She wished she hadn't called off of work just for a five-minute argument with this immature jerk.

"Hey whatever makes you happy," he replied. He took off his sunglasses again. "I'll call you later then."

I pursed my lips together. What was that supposed to mean? Why did he keep implying he wanted to talk to her? Where was he going with this? "Do you even have a job?" I asked, trying to hide how much he had irritated me.

"Yeah, I told you already, serial killer."

I stared at him. "Not funny," I snapped. I spun around and left the shop, leaving my barely touched-coffee on the table. As I passed the shop window, I saw Mr. Sam sitting by himself at our table. I let out a long breath of air. He was so enigmatic. Why couldn't I just control my temper and stay inside the shop a little longer? Maybe I wasn't good enough for him. That's why didn't work out on their not a date. Genie my ass.

Her heart jumped as she walked away from the building. It's stuff like that. You know? What right did he have? What kind of earnship? To think, making me fall in love with an idiot apparently wasn't a crime these days. Where were the police when you needed them?

I jumped into my car and turned on the radio. Love? Had she really just thought that? Was she already in love with him? Because that would be impossible. He was obnoxious and almost scary to her. They had nothing in common and he was obviously not attracted to her. So did that make him a potential soulmate? Definitely not.

So why was it that every time she thought about him she couldn't stop. He was not her type. He was not her type. He was not her type. She'd say it over and over again until this truth set her free.

I drove back to my apartment building and parked my car. Her non-date with Mr. Sam was the only thing she could think about. But who knew? Maybe he wasn't joking, to begin with. Maybe he really was a married serial killer. Or maybe he was just an asinine jerk like she thought originally.

I climbed out of my car and headed inside. I went into my apartment and sat down on the violet cushion couch. I looked for my phone in my purse. I wanted to call into work to try to get back on schedule. Because that was life you know. To finish one itinerary after another and never complain for a second that you had done something boring. It was just wrong. You know it? Just wrong.

Chapter 3

Beautiful bee
come sing to me
If he were half the man he said he was
I don't think I would've loved him as much
I'm tired of thinking that all this time I only saved one person's heart from heartbreak and it was mine
Do you ever wonder about things like that
Because to be perfectly honest
Guys like that come and go in dreams
because they're only real for one second or one weekend or maybe even in the years but that doesn't make him yours
so we build up the walls
to protect our feelings
and I must admit
I've never felt better before in my entire life

So I told my manager that I wasn't as sick as I thought and could maybe come into work but he assured me that it wasn't necessary and that I should stay home and recover anyway.

Complacent, I lay in my bed and moaned when a sharp pain in my brain threatened me with a headache. The morning sickness was wearing off from the night before, which was a good sign but I still had to close my curtains for what was left of it. I thought to myself about Mr. Sam. He was quite the character. She didn't know when the fine line between charming and annoying became an actual weapon but the point was that she was afraid he had seduced her. Let's just say the thought terrified me. First, it was coffee, next it would be full-blown beer and sex and I wasn't ready for any of that. I really wasn't.

I wasn't very popular in school, and not the least bit interesting enough to get bullied. I suppose you could've described me as invisible to everyone. I always wanted to be the main character of the story. Someone who could do that one little thing that charmed the world or something like that. I wanted to be able to write a great memoir of my life and put something other than, going home alone again, at the end of every chapter.

Later that day, I decided to go to the tavern I frequented every night and get something to drink. It was a little early for alcohol but I didn't care. I drove straight there and took a seat in my usual chair at the far end of the bar. The bartender Dave came straight up to me. "Christina, you're early. What's the occasion?"

"Just thirsty I guess." I dunno. It wasn't that big of a deal. I was just lonely maybe but I couldn't tell him that.

"The usual?"

"Yeah, thanks," I said.

Dave, my bartender was literally one of my few friends. It was kind of sad but I was used to sad things. I wasn't outgoing enough was my excuse. But what I really wanted was someone I could truly be myself around. I didn't have anyone like that at all in my life. The drama from meeting Mr. Sam was all she could think about now. Whatever, right?

Dave dropped two shots of whiskey in front of me and I slugged one back as quickly as possible. Mr. Sam crossed my mind more than just once as I drank and I couldn't figure out why. Was I making too big of a deal out of this? Probably.

I'm a therapist and I enjoy my job. I'm young and healthy and have my own apartment and car. My job pays well so I always have money to buy whatever I need. Why was I so insecure? I needed to be strong and confident. I had to become someone who could fall in love and be loved back in return. But if I didn't even have love for myself, how could I have it for someone else? Maybe I needed my own psychiatrist I could talk to. Someone who could explain to me what I was doing wrong.

I drank the second glass of whiskey and then put my head down on the bar table. I was such a loser. No wonder Mr. Sam didn't like me. If he liked me, he would've said something about it and he hadn't. I was going to die alone in my apartment and no one would come to my funeral.

I ordered another shot and a glass of water. I was starting to feel sick again. I looked around the near-empty tavern and realized no one would care even if I was sick. Feeling down, I drank my third shot and passed out in my chair, falling onto the ground.

When I woke up again, I was in the hospital. They had called an ambulance for me and I was now lying in a hospital room bed in the ER. I groaned from my splitting headache before passing out again.

I woke up the next morning. The doctor came into the room and explained to me what had happened. "Also," he said. "I see Dave is your only emergency contact."

"Yeah, he's my bartender," she mumbled.

"I see that. And when you drank that much, how did you expect to get home? You weren't going to drive, were you?"

I didn't answer. "Can I go? I'm going to be late for work."

"That's fine. You should be fine enough to leave. No drinking for the next couple of weeks. You were this close to an overdose." He smiled. "Take care."

I hurriedly left the hospital and drove to my job. I had already missed work because of stupid Mr. Sam the night before. I wasn't going to miss two days in a row. I got there just in time which was good news. The bad news was that I felt too sick to be there. I wanted to go home but I had to take things more seriously if I didn't want to lose what little I had already.

I went to work and sat down at my desk. My first patient came in and I felt relieved that everything was normal again and right where I had left it. "Good morning," I said cheerfully.

My patient's name was Jack Mullin and he was forty-four years old. He had schizophrenia and was currently unemployed and on disability. "Good morning Doctor," he said.

"And how are you feeling?" I asked him.

"Same as before," he mumbled. "The voices are less scary than before but they haven't gone away all the way yet."

"Have you been taking your medication?" I asked.

"Yes," he replied. "Which reminds me. I have a friend named Richard Phillips. He's a great guy and he's been going through some tough times. Would you be willing to take on another patient?" "Of course," I replied. "That'll be fine." oh, a new patient. She always enjoyed meeting new people. This should be interesting.

"He's really nice and he's been my friend for years now."

"I see," I replied. "How did you guys meet?"

"We met at a bowling alley. I was there with my cousin."

"Well tell him he's welcome to schedule an appointment with me," I said. "I'm looking forward to hearing from him."

"Great!" Jack said. "I told him all about you. You're an excellent doctor. That's why I referenced you."

"I'm flattered, thank you," I said.

We finished his session and I was thirsty so I went to the water fountain in the hall and filled my coffee mug with water. I took a sip and went back to my office. My next patient would be in at about a quarter after eleven which was about fifteen minutes from now. I took in a deep breath and let it out slowly.

My thoughts drifted off to dreaming about Mr. Sam. He was so forward and exciting. I was surprised he even spoke to me as much as he did.

She wondered, why people fall in love. Was it to defy the suffering of being lonely? Did it mean you were meant to be? Which poison could possibly justify the complexity of being in love with someone? I wasn't an expert at love. All crushes from school aside, I had pretty much never been in a mutually requited relationship before. It was a simple life but it had suited her just fine up until now.

When work was done with, she went back to her usual tavern and sat down at the bar. Dave greeted her. "You okay?" he asked.

"Yeah." "You blacked out. I'm glad to see you're okay," he said.

"Yeah, well I survived and I went to work anyway so I'm pretty happy. I'll have the usual."

"No thank you," Dave replied. He dropped a glass of water in front of her. "You can pick between this or cranberry juice. I'm not giving you a drop of alcohol."

I laughed a little. "I guess I can't talk you out of this?"

"No ma'am," he said.

"Fine, I'll take a cranberry juice."

"Perfect." He whipped up a glass of cranberry juice and set it in front of her. "How was work?" he asked.

"Pretty good," I said.

"Did you have trouble concentrating? You did just black out yesterday." He sounded concerned and I appreciated that.

“No, It was fine,” I said. “I got through the day.”

“I feel better now. I was worried about you.” He said.

“I’m okay now.” I sipped at my cranberry juice. “So how are the wife and kids?” I was desperate to change the subject. And maybe if she stuck around long enough he’d let her have some liquor.

“They’re good,” he replied. “My Son, Joseph, you know about Joseph don’t you?”

“The one in the fifth grade?”

“Yes. He just got his report card back. Straight A’s. Would you believe it? An A+ student. Nothing like his father. I never got good grades in school. I think a C- was my idea of a good job. Got held back a grade one time. I’m surprised I even managed to graduate. Anyway, the wife and I wanted to celebrate so we’re taking Joseph and Cindy to the amusement park this weekend. I’m really looking forward to it.”

“Oh, that’s great,” I said enthusiastically. “I’m glad to hear it.”

If she ever had a family. Would she even be able to do it? He made it sound so easy. She was happy for him that he was doing so well.

She left the bar when was done drinking her juice and talking to Dave. Her hangover was cured by aspirin and her self-consciousness was cured by a conversation with a friend. She got into her car and started the engine. For a moment, she found herself fantasizing about Mr. Sam. Would he ever marry her? Start a family. Have kinds. She knew it was farfetched but it was fun to think about. If they had kids what would their names be? Would they name a son after his father? She couldn’t even imagine what that would be like.

When she was done fantasizing, she pulled out of the tavern’s parking lot and began driving home.

Chapter 4

Simple now.
I still see you
even through frosted glass
Your word is golden
Your face is heaven
You scare me because I don't know what you want from me
In the end

Even in retrospect
I thought you'd be around for a little longer
Maybe that scared you away
because love is a candle
be careful
or it'll blow out
and we'll be left in the darkness of your heart
or even worse
the darkness of mine
Even if I can't say no to you
even if I can't go away without tears
even if the world goes crazy and we're the last people left
why did you leave
really
why did you leave
I just want to know what I did wrong.

So basically, I don't believe in miracles but now I'm not so sure. My cell rang about five minutes after she had gotten off of work. It was Mr. Sam again.

I didn't answer this time because I was still kind of mad at him. Then it rang three or four times and I gave up and answered his call. "Hello?"

"What made you run away the other day?"

"Nothing." I couldn't tell him about how insecure he had made her feel. If he was the sun then she was the moon and they were never meant to be together. But if I said all that he would probably think I was crazy so I kept it terse and to the point.

"If it was nothing then why didn't you stay?" He just had to ask, didn't he?

"What is this an interrogation?" I asked, sighing. The self-consciousness was returning. What did he care why she left anyway? It was almost none of his business. Mr. Sam was a puzzle boy and she was still having trouble figuring out what he wanted from her. If only there were a magical way to decode men. Wouldn't that be interesting?

"No," he said. "I'm not interrogating, I just want to know what upset you."

She couldn't tell if he was being serious or joking again so she took him seriously for once. "I just felt like leaving. I'm not going to make a big deal out of it."

"That's fine," he said. "It's not a problem. Then do you wanna stop by my place tonight? I'll make you dinner to make it up to you."

"No thank you. Once again," I said, growing tired of his jokes and forwardness. "Stop asking me." I didn't mean to be rude but I didn't trust him and I was afraid to let him into my heart. Love letters burn and marriage contracts can lead to divorce. There wasn't any other way around it. I just didn't know what I wanted anymore.

"I just want to see you again," he said finally.

"Why?" I asked. "I don't get it." He was persistent and she found that to be extraordinarily strange. Why did he want to get to know her so badly? Was this some kind of prank?

He answered, "Because you're cute. I'm cute. We're cute. It's simple science. When two people fall in love it's like that you know. It says so in the horoscopes. You do check your horoscopes, don't you?"

"Not really." When two people fall in love. Where'd he get that idea from? Was he ignoring everything I just said? He wasn't much of a listener. I wanted to cut the conversation short and hang up but something kept her on the phone.

"See that's your first problem. I don't know where I'd be without my morning forecast. It's good to keep up on that stuff. It'll make you lucky." He continued. "I know a great tarot card reader. She owns a little crystal shop. Wanna go with me? I'll take you some time."

"I really don't think…" I replied. I was losing the energy to argue with him. I didn't know if that was a good thing or a bad thing. He didn't seem to take no for an answer and that was never a good thing.

"Come on," he interrupted. "It'll be fun. I promise."

I had rejected him so much already that day that I was starting to get a guilty conscience again. What was the point of all this? She wasn't sure she wanted to end up on another no date, date. I ended up saying the last thing I ever thought I would say and it was "Sure I'll go." I almost snapped and took it back but his reply kept me silent.

"I'm so glad. We'll have so much fun. I'll pick you up tomorrow."

"Fine," I said. Was this seduction? Was Mr. Sam seducing me? Someone I couldn't say no to. Who in the world needed someone like that in their lives? But he was like her liquor, strong, sweet, and satisfying, and I felt like the seduction was taking over my body even now. It wouldn't be long before it took control of my nervous syndrome and turned me into a rabies patient.

I hung up the phone and yawned. It had been a long day and she was exhausted. I ran into a coworker on the way out. She was a cute girl in her twenties and had blond hair and blue eyes. She was a little taller than me and her name was Tracy.

"How did your day go?" she asked me.

"It was okay," I replied. Tracy didn't usually talk to me which made me bashful but she seemed nice when they followed each other out to their cars, I asked if she would like to go get lunch with me at the diner across the street.

She agreed and we both drove in separate cars to the restaurant. When they got there the hostess seated them at a table by the window. "You're always so shy. I'm surprised you wanted to hang out with me," she said.

"I've been going through a lot of weird stuff lately. I guess I was hoping you were someone I could talk to about it."

"Of course. I'm a good listener. What's on your mind." She asked.

"Well, there's this guy I met." "Oh no, boy problems," Tracy said. "Does this have a happy ending or a sad ending,"

"I don't know yet," I replied. "This guy is way out of my league. He's interesting and handsome and he's acting as if he's interested in me. But when I call him on it, he gets cold and rejects me. Do you think I should trust him?"

“Probably not. I haven’t trusted a man since my last ex-husband. He was a liar and I caught him cheating on me.”

“Oh no,” I said.

“As a general rule, I say never trust men. They’re hypocrites. They say one thing then do another. And they don’t know how to treat a woman.”

“That’s a little scary,” I admitted. But was she right? Was Mr. Sam an example of a man I couldn’t trust? How could she find out without getting her heart broken first?

The server appeared and we ordered our meals. He set down two glasses of iced tea, sweet for me, unsweetened for Tracy. When the server was gone, I continued, asking Tracy, “Do you think I should keep talking to this guy? I don’t want to get hurt by him.”

“Sometimes the best decisions we make in life require being alone. If you’re having doubts about him, you should probably break it off. Women’s intuition. We have it for a reason.”

“That makes sense,” I agreed.

“So what are you going to do about this guy?” she asked, leaning forward and sipping from her tea.

“I think I’m going to give him a chance,” I replied.

“Why?”

“I don’t know,” I replied. “I just want to figure out if we’re right for each other or not. I don’t know if he even thinks of me in that way. When I asked if we were on a date the other day, he told me no.”

Trish’s mouth fell into a straight line. “That’s what I’m talking about. Becoming obsessed with a jerk. You could do better but you won’t because you’re desperate.”

This was probably why I don’t hang out with people that often. I had low self-esteem and I hated it when people added to it. “I’m not desperate,” I muttered. “Why do you think I’m desperate.”

“Fine. I’m sorry. I shouldn’t have called you desperate but that’s my opinion and you wanted to know how I felt so now you know.” She sighed. “Hey, I have to break this dinner up a little short. I have to pick up my kids in daycare. Mind if I head out early? I’ll pay for my meal up at the register.” She picked up a coat and purse and left me alone at the table.

Great. Now she scared Tracy away. There was one thing she really needed to do before she got to know Mr. Sam any more than she already did. She was going to have to straighten herself out. Drop the self-conscious personality and move on from her past, no matter how sad it had been. I was ready to return to the world renewed and clean from her past and that would make things better and perfect and just how they always should've been. Right?

Chapter 5

I ran in a tragic circle
it defied gravity
it defied the stars
and it defied me
I don't want to pick you just because you're the only one left
When I fell
I fell so hard
that even the ground couldn't break my fall
And when I finally hit the bottom of the well
the water was my only solace
and relief washed over me
it was just a dream
why are dreams like that sometimes?

There was a song I heard in a dream I had. It wasn't quite a nightmare or a normal dream. Just words to a song I heard while I lay in an imaginary dream bed. Anyway, I woke up a little late and now I had to hurry and get to work, not to mention the tarot reading I had to get to after work with Mr. Sam. I ran to my car and drove to work. It was a quiet building of therapists like me with a business manager that we called boss. My first client for the day was a stout man with a mustache who was never nice to me. I don't know why he is so rude to me but I guess to each his own.

"Well David Morgan you're early, aren't you," she said to him.

He looked at his watch and frowned. "No. You're just late. You have no idea how much I need this session right now. It's something of an emergency if you don't mind."

"Of course," I replied. "Step inside my office and take a seat. Would you like a bottle of water? I can go grab you one."

"No. I don't want water, I want you to do your job and give me my therapy session."

"No problem." This close, by the way. This close to telling this guy to bug off. But then again, I am a professional and professionals don't give up just because their client is obnoxious. "So now," she began taking a seat behind her desk and computer.

"What seems to be the problem?"

"My problem," he snapped. "Is that nothing ever goes right? I think it's going right and then it doesn't. I try to be decent. Does anyone ever look at me and say 'Hey that's a decent guy over there'? No never and you know why?"

"Why?"

"Because the system is corrupt. I'm not the only one that has noticed it."

"And have you been taking your pills?" I asked

"No, because it protects the system. Even you. I don't know if I should trust you. How do I know what's in those pills you prescribed to me? For all I know it's poison."

"I can assure you it's not poison. It'll help calm your nerves, is all."

"Treat my nerves. My nerves are the last thing I need to treat. I need answers doc. What can you tell me to make me feel less like I'm going out of my mind."

I ask, "Have you been sleeping well?"

"No."

"David, I'm afraid you might be suffering from paranoid schizophrenia. Have you noticed any voices or had any trouble making basic observations?"

"You think I'm crazy."

"I don't think you're crazy. I just want to help. Now Abilify which is a treatment for schizophrenia just made its generic version go live. It used to be quite expensive and hard to get a hold of but the generic is quite reasonably priced and you can pick it up at any drugstore pharmacy."

"I will not be silenced."

"I'm here to help you, not silence you."

"Fine, I'll try the Abilify."

I almost thought he would jump out of his chair and pull a Mr. Sam and say he was just joking but he looked quite serious. Smiling, I wrote out his prescription and gave it to him. I'll call the pharmacy ahead of time and let them know you're coming. You still get your meds at CLUB pharmacy on Bishop.

"Yes."

"Perfect. We'll monitor you and see if you need anything in the future."

When the therapy session was over, I went to get a glass of water before my next patient came in. The one that my patient Jack Mullin had referenced to me, Richard Phillips. And that was when it happened. I sat at my desk and a young man came in. He was tall, blonde, and from the looks of his file, the same age as me. Despite his gorgeousness, I kept it professional because I was good at it and asked what he would like to talk about.

He replied. "I don't feel happy." He gave a crooked smile. "Not to be a bummer or anything."

"Why do you think that is?" I asked him, trying to concentrate on what he was saying and not on his face.

"I don't know. It started about a year ago and never went away. I'm just constantly never happy."

Was he single? She doubted it. He was perfect. She didn't know there were even guys like him out there. I stared at him blankly before asking finally, "Were there any triggers perhaps? A marriage? A Funeral? A breakup. Loss of job…."

"No. Nothing like that. I'm just a sad, depressing person, I guess."

Her heart beat in her chest and she realized she was almost as sympathetic on a personal level as she was on a professional level. It felt like she had known him for years and were best friends or something. I wanted to know more about him but thought it was ethically wrong so I said instead, "Well I can prescribe you some Prozac if you're interested in trying it."

"I don't know. I've tried medicine like that before and it never worked. I don't think."

"Hmmm, well tell me more. Is there anything else I should know?" His demeanor was so gentle. He looked like a puppy. For some reason, she could already tell that this person was very kind and considerate.

He smiled at me again which I found strange considering his depression. "I just have to ask. Would you ever go out to dinner with me?"

I froze. Did I do something wrong? Or something right? What the hell was going on with all these supermodel guys? Did they get fed up with their supermodel wives or what? Why was everyone asking her out all of a sudden?

"I don't date my patients," I blurted out finally. It was true and the best I could do at the time considering my circumstances.

"No problem. Just thought I'd ask."

"Good then. We're agreed."

"I don't mean to pry," I began reluctantly. "But why do you want to go on a date with me? Or were you just joking"

"I dunno," He said. "I guess I just like you. You're nice to talk to."

"Oh, I see. Well, thank you for the compliment."

"No problem," he said. "But that leads to the obvious question?"

"What's that?" I asked.

"Why did you reject me?"

I shook my head. "I have a date today is all. I need to see where it goes before I do anything differently."

"That's okay then," he said quickly. "I guess I'm not too good with women."

I smiled at him. "Yeah well, you obviously don't need to look very hard. You're a pleasure, Richard."

"Thank you." He paused. "Well, I told you all my secrets. Now you tell me yours. What's bothering you? You don't look super thrilled. Plus you have a date. Shouldn't you be happy?"

"I'm plenty happy Richard. I'm looking forward to my date." "I guess," he said shrugging. "Just thought I'd check."

I smiled at him. "Thanks for asking though. I appreciate that."

With the prescription written and all else done, Richard left the office and I went to the restroom. In the restroom, I stared into the mirror. Why was everyone asking me out lately? Was it some kind of joke they were playing on me? Sighing, I left the restroom and went back to my office. I

had about three more clients that day and I didn't have time for frivolous thoughts about the male psyche.

I ran into Tracy as I was leaving work. I caught up to her and said, "Sorry I scared you away yesterday."

Tracy looked at her. "No worries. I'm sorry I called you desperate. I didn't mean it. I just think about guys like that and it frustrates me."

"I understand," I said. "Well, I'm just glad you're not mad at me." Which she meant. Her failed attempt at friendship with Tracy was still embarrassing but at least they weren't mad at each other. Although it did add to her loneliness. Why was she so bad at relationships? It was frustrating and painful.

"Of course. I'm not that petty," She said. She reached her car. "I'll see you tomorrow."

"Okay, Bye," I said. I went to my car and got in. I was nervous about my date with Mr. Sam. Was it a date this time? She wasn't sure. She couldn't believe she was going to see him again. She thought about Mr. Sam as she drove back to her place. She thought it was strange that she thought about him so much. For a split second, the conversations between her and Richard popped into her head. She shook away the memory and went back to thinking about her date.

When she got home, she fixed herself something to eat. She had skipped lunch that day and now she was starving. She put together a bowl of salad and some cottage cheese. Then she sat down at her dining room table and began to eat her food. It wouldn't be long before her date with Mr. Sam and she didn't want anything to get in the way, including feeling hungry. No distractions. No running away. No vomiting on him. Tonight was going to be perfect. She wouldn't have it any other way.

My phone rang and it was my foster mom. "Hi honey," she said.

"Oh Mom," I said in surprise. "How are you?"

"I just called to make sure you were okay. I heard from your bartender that you passed out and were sent to the hospital. Is that true?"

"Yeah, it was something like that," I admitted.

"I told you about drinking too much. You're going to give yourself liver cancer if you don't calm down."

"I'm not going to get liver cancer from a few drinks."

"And for that matter," her foster mother continued. "How come you never call? I know you're busy with work but surely you have time to give your father and me a call once in a while."

"Sorry," I said. "I'll call more often." She probably wouldn't. They were good to her growing up but she could never get past the feeling of being with strangers when she was with them. It made her nervous being alone with them. She didn't know why she never felt quite comfortable with her family. Maybe she was just a bad person.

"What are you doing right now, anyway," Her foster mother said. "Have you been eating? You're so skinny. You make me worry about you."

"I just ate a few minutes ago." "What did you eat?"

"A Salad and cottage cheese," I said.

"That's not enough food, dear. You need to eat some meat. It would be good for you."

"I'm a vegetarian, remember?"

"I try to forget. Why don't you come over for dinner tonight? It would do you some good to be with the family."

I replied. "I can't. I have a date."

"A date," her foster mother said. "A date with you."

"A guy named Sam. I met him a few days ago."

"Is he safe to be around? You just met him."

"Yes, he's safe," I replied. "I've hung out with him a few times now."

"Well invite him over for dinner too. It would be nice if we could meet him."

"Maybe another time," I promised. "We're just going to go out to get our tarot cards read. I don't think we'll make it over to your place in time."

"Tarot cards?" my foster mother said. "No witchcraft. It's unchristian. He better be Christian. Is he Christian?" I sighed. "I don't know mom, I didn't ask him."

"Well let me know when you do."

"I have to go, Mom. He's going to be here soon." I said.

"Alright fine. Goodnight dear. Don't be a stranger."

I got off the phone with my foster mom and went into the bathroom to get ready for my date.

Chapter 6

I figured as much
it doesn't matter how much you cry
it doesn't bring him back
I think I'm tired of feeling sorry for myself
I was happy because you liked me
And I was happy because you didn't
I wish I had known that earlier
you were so full of it sometimes

I didn't pretty myself up for my evening with Mr. Sam. Okay, I'm lying. I wore my barely used red lipstick and the blackest black mascara. I don't want to say I did all that to impress him. I do want to think I did it for my own well-being. So that's my final statement on that.

I wasn't sure what to expect from tonight. Anything could happen. And I just had to keep him from trying to have sex with me and we'd be gold. I was positive his seduction powers had a limit and I was getting to know him better so I should be becoming immune to his advances any time now.

He pulled up and I climbed into his convertible with the top down. The sun was setting and left the sky a cotton candy pink.

"You look nice," was the first thing he said to me.

"Thank you," I replied. I didn't expect the compliment but I appreciated it.

"So ready to get your fortune told?" he asked me.

"I guess so," I said. He turned onto the next street and we drove in silence for about ten minutes before I finally asked where the crystal store was located. "How far away is this place again?"

He pulled onto a country road and began to speed up. "An hour away," he replied. "This is a shortcut."

I felt more and more annoyed the faster he drove. "What are you doing? Why are we driving so fast?"

"Because it's fun," he replied. "Why else?"

"You're joking," I complained. "You're going to crash and get us killed."

"I'm not worried. I drive like this all the time."

I felt my muscles tense up, almost preparing myself for any kind of car accident that could happen at any time now. This was ridiculous. Mr. Sam had zero driving skills. He made a sharp turn down another road and began to drive even faster.

"I'd like to get there in one piece," I complained.

"Lighten up," he said with a smile. He turned the radio on and an eighties pop song turned on. He began to sing out loud. "Have a good time. It goes like this," he said. He put his left hand up and began dancing in his seat. He sang his heart out and pumped his left fist to the beat.

I stared at him. Maybe he was right. Maybe this was fun. What did I know about fun? I couldn't even remember the last time I'd had a really great time doing anything at all. Was this what I secretly wanted? Was this a world I was even allowed to enter at my age? I wasn't sure about anything anymore. All I knew was that if Mr. Sam could do it, I could do it better. I lifted both my hands up, catching wind and fresh air in his topless convertible. I began to sing with the music too and pumped both my fists in the air. It was exhilarating.

"There you go," he exclaimed. "Now you're getting the hang of it."

When I was younger, maybe in college, I had dreamed of being an outgoing and more open person. Maybe now, ten years later, maybe I was getting my chance. We drove for about an hour and fifteen minutes singing and dancing in the car to blasting music. When we got there my hair was a bee's nest on top of my head and I made a futile effort to comb it back down with my fingers.

We pulled into a small parking lot in front of the crystal shop. "We're here," Mr. Sam said. "Let's go in. I called and told them we were coming."

We went inside and I was surprised by how beautiful the shop was. Each shelf was stocked with brightly colored crystals, incense, and dried herbs.

"Greetings," the cashier said cheerfully. "I'm Nichole. Jennifer is in the back. She will read your tarot cards."

Mr. Sam took my hand and led me to the back. We pushed back a beaded curtain and found Jennifer sitting at a table and playing on her iPhone. She looked up at us and put down her phone. “Finally Sam,” she complained. “You’re late. I almost left.”

“Glad you didn’t. This is Christina. She’d like to have her tarot cards read.”

“Well no harm done,” she sighed. “Have a seat.” She gestured to the chairs in front of her table. We both sat down. Then she pulled out a deck of tarot cards from a flannel drawstring pouch. She shuffled them a few times before asking “Now what is your first question?”

I thought about it for a while before asking “Will I get a raise at work?”

Jennifer placed several cards on the table, analyzing them carefully. “I see something special about your job but I don’t see anything about money. The cards are telling me to encourage you to keep working there though. It will be a good thing later. You’ll see.” She looked up at me. “Next question?”

“Will I ever be happy?” I asked after a moment’s hesitation. Mr. Sam looked at me and so did Jennifer. Maybe that question was awkward. “I’m sorry. Should I ask a different question?”

“No, it’s fine. I can answer that for you.” She reshuffled her cards and laid them out on the table in front of her. “Don’t worry I’ve heard and seen it all before.” She stared at the cards. “I see a twin star in the sky. He’s the one that will make you happy.”

“Oh,” Mr. Sam interrupted enthusiastically, “Am I the twin star.”

“Um sure,” Jennifer said. “Why not? Perhaps.”

“See, I’m good luck,” Mr. Sam said. “You gotta stick around me and I’ll make you happy.”

“I see,” I mumbled.

“So Sam told me a little about you,” Jennifer said. “How did you two meet again?”

“We met at a bar I go to every night,” I replied.

“Yeah she threw up on me,” he said.

I felt my cheeks flush. “Yeah, I drank a little too much. I told him I could give him some money to pay for a new pair of pants but he said no.” She gestured towards Mr. Sam. “How do you two know each other?”

“We went to the same college together,” she said. “We dated for about a week too. It was a disaster.” “Yeah, I thought she was going to kill me when I cheated on her.”

“You cheated on her?” I asked.

"Yeah," he said. "Forbidden fruit. She and I had just started dating when the new girl in school hit on me. She joined our class two weeks late. She was beautiful. I couldn't say no."

"Makes you think, doesn't it," Jennifer said. "Sam's not exactly what I'd call reliable. But he's got a good heart. I guess you'll find out when you get to know him better."

"Alright. Enough gossiping about me," Sam interrupted. "Read my cards next."

"Okay, sure," she said. She put the cards in a pile and began shuffling them again. "What do you want to ask me?"

"Will I ever fly to outer space," he asked.

Jennifer rolled her eyes. "Serious questions only please."

"I am being serious." Sighing Jennifer laid out eight cards. "Fine." She looked across the cards and pointed to the four wands. "You are going to have a dream that you're in outer space but it's just a dream," she said.

Sam frowned. "That's no good. Try again. Tell me when I'll see outer space."

Sighing again even louder, Jennifer laid out two more cards. "Yes, you'll definitely go to outer space." she agreed.

"When?" he asked.

"Tomorrow," she replied flatly.

"Perfect!" he exclaimed. "Now we're getting somewhere."

I began chuckling and covered my mouth to hide it. Mr. Sam could be so funny at times. "Am I going to outer space too?" she asked, jokingly.

"Yes," Jennifer replied. "You're both going tomorrow." She paused. "Okay serious questions only from now on," she said. She looked at me. "What else do you want to know?"

I thought about it before answering. Hmmm, what should she ask? She said finally, "will I meet a best friend."

"Like a dog?" Mr. Sam asked.

"No. Not like a dog," she replied. "Like a bff. A girl I can talk to about boys and stuff."

"Okay, let me see." Jennifer shuffled her cards and laid them out. "I do see friendship blossoming. Not too long from now. She will appreciate you for you and you'll be able to tell her anything."

"Will I know when I meet her?" she asked.

"Yes. You'll be able to tell right away." Jennifer answered.

I wanted that to be true.

"Sam, would you like a new reading?"

"Yes," he replied.

Jennifer shuffled the deck. "Okay. Go ahead. What would you like to know."

"Will my parents ever respect me?"

Jennifer laid out eight cards and replied. "I'm seeing a lot of friction," she said. "I think the respect will come but you might have to do something."

"Do something. Like what?" he asked.

"Like get married and have kids. That is the only way you'll earn their respect."

"I'm not doing that," he groaned. He looked at Jennifer. "You are the opposite of a good fortune teller."

She frowned. "Hey, I don't control the cards. They speak and I listen. It's very simple logic."

"I don't care. I need better answers. Do Christina again. It's her turn."

"I can't think of any more questions," I said.

"Think of something. Anything. I want to get my dollars' worth." "How much was this?" I asked. For some reason, I had thought this was a free session between friends.

"A hundred dollars."

Jennifer said, "How do you think I could put up with him otherwise." She turned to me. "Okay, last question. What do you want to know?"

I thought again but no matter how I racked my brain I couldn't think of a question. I finally asked, "Is this a date."

Jennifer looked at Sam. He was leaning back in his chair, head back and eyes closed. He waved his hand. "You can tell her yes."

Jennifer turned to me again. "Yes, this is a date."

"Okay thank you." I felt relieved. I had been scared to ask Mr. Sam herself because she didn't want to be rejected again.

"All right. We're closing up the store for the night." She sat up and put her cards back into their pouch. "You guys gotta G O go."

"Thanks for the reading," I said, standing up as well. "It was fun." Mr. Sam said. "I told you, you'd like it. I'm the king of thinking of fun things to do."

"I suppose you're right," I said.

With the tarot reading done, we went back to the car and began to drive back to my place. Mr. Sam took us down the same country road and turned up the radio once more. We danced in our seats and held our arms high up in the air. I even began to sing along with him. It was the most fun I think I have ever had in one day.

When we got back to my place around 9 pm, Mr. Sam asked. "May I come in?"

"Not tonight," I said.

"But I'm good luck," he complained.

"I suppose."

He continued. "She said I was your twin star."

"Even so."

"I like you very much."

"That's fine too," I said. "But I'm tired and I still have no intention of letting you into my apartment."

He sighed loudly. "Please."

"No thank you." I stopped myself and was beside myself when I said. "Perhaps another night. Not tonight. But maybe another night. When I trust you a little bit more."

"Okay," he said smiling. "If it's for you, I can wait. Forever even. Just let me know." He gave a quick wave goodbye, jumped back into his car, and sped off.

"Forever huh," I mumbled. "Kinda long isn't it."

Chapter 7

I left you for the world
maybe if I wasn't so petty
we'd be together now
I never stopped loving you
I just never want to see you again

Believe it or not, I fell asleep on the couch. I mean, literally, I never fell asleep on my own couch before. And definitely never fell asleep on my couch for an entire night. But I was exhausted and couldn't make it to my room. I woke up because of my cell phone ringing. I picked it up. It was Mr. Sam. "Hello?"

"Did you just wake up?" he asked.

"Yeah," I replied. "Why?"

"Aren't you supposed to be at work?"

My eyes widened. "Oh shoot. What time is it?"

"Ten," he said.

Great. She had slept in. "I was supposed to be there at nine. I gotta run. Thanks for calling."

I hung up on him before he could say another word, grabbed my purse, and headed out the door. I got there as soon as possible and was officially one and a half hours late. My manager called. "Christina, what's going on with you? Why are you late?"

"I slept in. I'm sorry. It won't happen again."

"Your patient Josh Zimmeron is still waiting for you in your office. Hurry and get to him before he leaves."

"Yes of course. Thank you." I said. I went to my third-floor office and saw Josh Zimmeron just as he was putting his coat back on.

"Josh," I said quickly hurrying in. "I'm here, Sorry I was late. You can go into my office."

She joined him in her office and sat down. Enough goofing off. She had to get serious again or she was going to lose her job. Mr. Sam was fun but she had her limits. At least he woke her up when he called. Who knew how late she'd be if it weren't for him?

"So what would you like to discuss today?" I asked finally, positioning myself over my computer.

"My girlfriend just broke up with me. I don't know what made her want to leave. I thought we were in love." "I see."

He continued. "I thought we'd move in together. Get married eventually. You know, start a family. The American dream."

"Yes, I see," I replied.

"And the worst thing about it, the thing that really got to me…"

"What was that?" I asked.

"Is that she didn't even look sad when she broke up with me? Not a tear. She didn't even care that I was falling apart inside. She made me feel like I did something wrong. I didn't do anything to justify this type of breakup." He started crying and I didn't know what to say.

"You'll find the right person for you," I said finally. "She just wasn't the one." "You think so?"

"I know so." She pulled up his medicine record on her computer. I felt bad for him. He looked really upset. I wasn't sure what to say to him. Relationships need both hearts to power love. What were you supposed to do when you were the only one contributing? "Did she say why she left?"

"No. I think she found someone else. That's my guess anyway?"

"That's really sad," I agreed. "I know you'll be able to get through this. You're a strong guy. You can do it."

"I guess so," he mumbled. "Could I have a tissue?"

I reached for the tissue box on my desk, grabbed a tissue, and handed it to him.

"Thanks," he said, dabbing at his eyes.

I felt bad for him but I didn't know how to make him feel better so I continued, "How are the meds working for you anyway? Have you been taking them?"

"Yeah, I take them."

"Do you think if you had an increase in Prozac, you'd feel better?"

He paused, taking a moment to reply. "You know what?"

"What?"

"I think I'll pass. I'm just going to cry it out of my system. I don't need a pill for that."

"That's fine," I agreed. "Just let me know if you change your mind. We'll keep your meds the same then."

"Thank you."

I got through all my patients. I was exhausted from the night before and I barely made it through the day.

Later on, I got home from work at about 6 pm. I took a shower, brushed my teeth, and changed into sweats. I sighed. I felt like the worst was over. I just wanted to crawl into bed early and read a good book for a couple of hours before going to sleep. I had never been so irresponsible in my entire life. Imagine me, being late for work. I almost couldn't believe it myself.

I was just about to start reading when my cell rang. I checked to see who it was and it was Mr. Sam. Him again? I answered the phone. "Hello?"

"Hey, Christina. Did you get to work okay?"

"Yes, I did thank you."

"Wanna go out for dinner or something?"

"I can't. I'm already in bed."

"So early?"

I sighed. "yeah so early."

"Why in the world would you ever be in bed so early."

"I'm reading."

"Well, I have something way more fun than that in mind. Wanna hang out?"

"I'm not sure." This guy had unlimited energy. Didn't he have anything else important to do? I stared at the book in my hands. It might be kind of fun to change up her usual routine for something more exciting.

He said, "Maybe I could take you out for dinner and a movie?"

I felt like I was eternally fighting off his seduction. What did he want from me, anyway? To be liked. To be loved. What was he talking about? "It's a weekday. I can't. I have work in the morning. I can't be late again."

"Come on. It'll be fun. I can be at your place in ten minutes."

I wondered what to make of all his invitations. Would it be a good idea to take him up on his offer for dinner and a movie? Was this her chance to change up her monotonous routine in life and do something different?

When I was five, right before the accident that took my mother's and my father's life, I told my mother I wasn't able to make any friends in school. She told me to never give up and that someday I'd meet a special someone, a special friend who would keep me from being lonely. She promised me that love was the greatest gift of all and not to be scared to wait for it. "It'll just happen," she said. "Just like that."

"Just like that," I muttered. "Just like what?"

"Ugh," I groaned. Why not? Maybe this was the friend that my mother had promised me all those years ago. "Fine," I replied finally. "I'll go out with you."

"Great. Meet you at your place." Like it was easy. He said everything like it was easy and implied and never seemed to doubt his own decisions. The things that were exhausting for me were like nothing to him. I had no idea what he saw in me. We obviously had nothing in common.

"Bye," I said and hung up.

I got out of bed and dressed myself in a long-sleeved teal dress that made me look fat. Then I put on some flats and lipstick and was ready to go. I don't know why I agreed to the date. He was borderline driving me crazy with all his unlimited energy and personality. But you know, I liked him. A lot. I wanted to see him again and from the sounds of it, he wanted to see me again too. It was too early in the game to call him my crush or idol but I was definitely starting to feel something in my chest at the mere mention of him.

Life was always so routine to me. You know. You wake up shower and dress. You go to work from nine to five. You come home, eat, drink, sleep. Easy. It was a simple itinerary that I had done all by myself. Because when I thought about it, perhaps what made this world of mine so boring was the fact that I had spent a very large chunk of it completely alone. I had no friends, and no family because they died in the boating accident. Funny how you remember the little things when it's tragic. I had no one and never spent one day regretting it. I just existed only. Doing something was all I had and I had done it a lot.

If this is life, give me more. I don't know how to explain my heart. It wanted to be left alone. It was almost as if the only excitement in her life was to talk to her patients and live her life through their problems. I'm not sure why

I never noticed that before. Maybe I wanted to be seen. Now that I had found a friend or whatever Mr. Sam was to me, I could be happy. I could be a person capable of happiness. Capable of love.

Mr. Sam arrived at my apartment building and I went into his car.

The restaurant they went to was a simple one. They served mostly sandwiches, cheeseburgers, and fries. Mr. Sam was trying to convince me to get the double bacon cheeseburger.

"Their burgers are out of this world!" he exclaimed. "They're so good here."

"I'm a vegetarian," I replied.

"One time won't kill you."

"I'm watching my weight," I said lamely.

"Come on. Try it." He insisted. When he insisted, the seduction took over like a virus and I couldn't say no to him. "Don't they have some kind of vegetable alternative to meat? I could get a veggie burger if they had one."
"Even if they had one I wouldn't let you get it. Come on, try the cheeseburger. A little beef is good for you, once in a while."

I sighed. To be honest, it wasn't the fat content of the meat I was worried about, which burgers had a lot of. And it wasn't that I don't normally eat meat, which I don't. And I'm not a complete vegetarian because I do like seafood and this was not seafood. The truth was that I had a safe space and Mr. Sam was invading it. I kept giving in to him and I wasn't sure why I was doing that.

I finally gave up and ordered the bacon cheeseburger. The food came out pretty quickly so that was good. I took a bite of my burger, chewing slowly and not enjoying it the least bit. This was disgusting. She hadn't had red meat since she was twelve. Mr. Sam didn't seem to care that I was suffering and that annoyed me greatly. I had to stop giving in to him. But how?

Mr. Sam was the king of small talk. All he did was talk. He talked about skiing in the alps and his yacht in the pacific. He said he had been to Spain twice for vacation and England once. He said the casinos in Canada could really rip a hole in your pocket. He talked so much in fact I almost stopped listening because his stories were probably not true.

"And that's why," he said, finishing off his monologue. "That's why I never went to that restaurant again."

"How do you afford all these things?" I asked. I wasn't trying to bully him, I was just confused about him. "Do you even work?"

"Yes, I work. I'm an explorer."

"That's not a job."

"It is. I do it constantly. I'll even bring you along and show you what I've seen."

"What does it pay?"

"It's not about money. It's not about having a paying job, you know?"

"How can you afford all these adventures then?"

"Easy. My parents are rich."

"Ah." That explained it. From his spoiled brat attitude to his Hollywood tan, she should've figured as much.

"What about you?" he asked

"What about me, what?"

"What do you do?"

"I told you I'm a therapist. That is what I do."

"No, not what you do for money, what do you do?"

I wasn't sure what to say so I blurted out the first thing that came to mind. "I'm a single woman and I'm already twenty-nine and I've never even kissed anyone let alone slept with them. I don't have any dating history and I live alone. Fine. You got it out of me. Now what?" He was making me expose myself and I wasn't sure I was comfortable with it. I liked my privacy. I needed it to breathe but Mr. Sam kept digging and I kept giving him whatever he wanted.

"I think I like you more now," he said smiling. "I'm glad you felt like you could tell me that." He continued. "So maybe you'll let me be your first kiss?"

"I don't know," I said with a sigh. "I don't want to talk about it anymore."
"Why not?"

"Because it's embarrassing and private and I don't know why I told you."

"It's fine. I can listen."

The bills came and he paid for both of them. This was probably a date too. I didn't ask because I didn't want to be rejected again but I was flattered by the company. We went to the movie theater and I was surprised when he pulled out two movie tickets.

"When did you have time to buy those?"

"I bought them before I came to get you."

"What movie are we watching?"

“It’s an action movie. the one with Thomas Jack in it. You’ll like it. It got rave reviews.”

“Hmmm. Okay,” I agreed. “Sounds good to me.”

They went into the movie theater and sat down by each other. He didn’t put a finger on her which she preferred and secretly appreciated. The movie starts off with a house exploding, set off by the main character. The movie wasn’t her type but she was actually starting to like it. A beautiful woman in the movie grabbed the main character and pulled him in closer. When they were just inches away, they had a moment and kissed passionately.

This made me look towards Mr. Sam. Would I ever kiss Mr. Sam? Or better even, would Mr. Sam ever kiss me?

When the movie was over, Mr. Sam drove me home and I was dizzy from the exciting film. He parked in front of my apartment and looked at me, puckering up. “Hollywood kiss before you go babe?” he asked.

I stared at him before smiling. “Not yet. I’m not ready. Can you wait?”

“Forever and ever,” he said. “Just like I promised.”

“Okay,” I said. “Thank you.” I turned away from him and headed back to my apartment.

Chapter 8

what if the stars weren't real
just optical illusions from the sun and moon That's how I feel about you
You shine so bright
are you just a dream?
Heartbreak
If it weren't for you
I don't think I even would've bothered Keep shining star
Even if it's not for me.
Keep shining and I'll watch from the distance alone
just know it
I only let go
because that's how much I loved you

Mr. Sam called me again to my surprise, right as I was getting off of work. He has called me every day so far since I met him a couple of weeks ago. "Hi," he said.

"Hi," I replied.

"Can I come over?"

"Not today."

"Wanna hang out?" he asked.

I thought about it. "Maybe."

"Come over to my place?"

"No thank you."

He offered, "Dinner?"

I was a little hungry. Dinner might be nice. "Sure."

"Great. See you in a half hour."

That didn't give her much time to get ready. "Okay that's fine," I said.

He hung up and I threw on a white spring dress. I put on red lipstick and mascara. I grabbed my purse and waited for Mr. Sam to call me to let me know that he was here. I don't usually dress like this but I was starting to like Mr. Sam as more than a friend and I felt the unexplainable desire to try and impress him.

When he arrived, I went outside and climbed into his convertible. The top was down again and he turned the radio up as loud as it would go. We danced in our seats and threw our hands up to the beat of the music. We arrived at the restaurant and he opened the door for me before we went inside. The greeter set us up a table by the window in the back of the restaurant.

"So you're a vegetarian," he said.

I guess he was listening. I was glad to hear that. Especially after making her eat an entire burger made from cows. "Yes, but I do like fish once in a while."

"They have a great seafood selection here," he said, showing me his menu. "Have you ever had a shark?"

I shook my head. "Does a shark count as a fish?"

"Yeah of course it does," he replied.

"Have you ever eaten a shark before?" I asked.

"Twice. From here. It was so good."

"Okay I'll try it," I agreed. "It sounds interesting."

The server appeared and we both ordered. Shark for me and T-bone steak for him. She liked how Mr. Sam made her feel like trying new things. Never in a million years would she have expected to behave as she had since she had met Mr. Sam. And she liked it. She liked the new her.

As usual, Mr. Sam was a wonderful conversationalist. He managed to talk the entire time there and never got bored. I wanted to be like that too. Someone who could hold a conversation on their own and never get tired. "You've experienced so much," I commented.

"Yes, well like I told you before I'm an adventurer. I like discovering new things and new people." He smiled at me. "Like you. I met you and that was an adventure in itself. I enjoy your company and that's what's important."

"You think I'm an adventure?" I laughed.

"Yes. We're just living in a dream you know. Nothing's real until we say it is. I think that's my favorite part about it. We never know whether we're awake or asleep. We just do things and they happen. Like magic. I think life is full of surprises and experiences."

"I wish I could be that way too," I sighed. "But I feel old and like I don't know whether I'm coming or going. You've helped me see that it's possible to find happiness at any time in life."

"That's what I'm talking about. Trust. It's all about trust and dreaming. What do you like the most about your job, for example?"

"I like helping people. I like feeling like I've made a difference in someone's life."

He replied. "But don't forget your own. You worry about everyone's problems but your own. You need to think of yourself too. It would be good for you."

"I suppose," I replied. I blushed and he put his hand on mine.

"Just stay open to new things and it'll all make sense later."

"Thank you. That means a lot to me." I said. I was starting to see things differently. Each story he told touched my heart and I wondered if this was what love felt like. Was she in love? Was she even capable of receiving the kind of love he could give?

He was so excited and she herself was borderline boring. But she liked him. To put it simply she liked him.

I put the most painful memories behind me. Losing my parents for example. I put my best moments forward and tried to stitch it up like a doll. I wanted to be a full-blooded queen but I was too scared to accept myself for who I was. I wanted to be happy too. I wanted to be like Mr. Sam, full of energy and spontaneity. Was it possible for Mr. Sam to like me back? Could he fill the emptiness in my heart, the hole that had grown bigger and bigger her whole life from neglect and pessimism? I wanted to think that maybe that was possible.

We finished dinner. The food was delicious. The company was good. And the bill was covered as if we were on a date.

Was it a date? She wasn't sure. She didn't want to jump to conclusions again. It would be way too embarrassing, and she didn't want to ask because she didn't want him to know how much she cared. Why is it that the things we love the most are the things we talk about the least?

"I could've gotten that," said finally.

"It's not a problem," he said.

My heart skipped a beat. Was he thinking what she was thinking? She couldn't tell. Was it too early to tell him she wanted to see him again… and again… and again?

We left the restaurant and he dropped me back off at my apartment. As he drove away, I found myself fantasizing about things that didn't happen and things that probably never would. I went into my apartment and decided I had made the right decision to go out with him that night.

Chapter 9

You're like wine
You're like drugs
you're like candy
but most of all
you're like poison
and I want to die in your arms
from too much of you.

Every so often I think of you again.
No wonder I feel so bad
I never regretted before you
I suppose that's my freedom

I went to work the next morning in high spirits. I was really starting to like Mr. Sam. He was exciting. He was crazy and wild. I wanted to know everything about him and at the same time, I wanted him to have his secrets. She felt happy spending time with him and wanted more.

A long time ago, I had a crush on my classmate in high school. I loved him so much and told my best friend at the time, a small girl even mousier than me, that I liked him. We kept it our secret that I liked him. He was handsome and had a good sense of humor. Every day he would pass by my desk to his desk one seat behind me and I would think that he smelled like peppermint and sweat. He was the star of the football team and he was very popular with pretty much everyone.

One day he asked to borrow my pencil. I was thrilled because he had never spoken one word to me before that day. When he was finished with it towards the end of class, he handed it back to me. The pencil was special now. As a matter of fact, I think I still have it somewhere in a box at my apartment. But the point is he made me very happy that day. My only regret is that the pencil became the one and only interaction between us for the rest of high school.

Despite all that, the crush was fun and kept me busy. I wonder if that's why I never had a boyfriend. As if I was waiting for him forever. But forever came and went and now I'm here and I don't even remember what he looked like. His face faded with time as time does and I will forever remember him for what he was. A pleasant dream I had that one time.

Was Sam going to be like that too? That person I met before but never again? The guy I wanted forever but never had my feelings returned. She didn't want to think about it but it was bothering her. Temporary alliance dates, do those even count?

I met with my first patient for the day, "Good morning Miller," I greeted. "And how are we feeling today."

"More of the same," he sighed, seated in front of my desk. "My wife left me. She was having an affair and she left me for him."

I frowned. "I'm so sorry to hear that. Would you like to talk about it?"

"Yeah. I spent thousands on my wife. I bought her jewelry and shoes and whatever else she wanted and she betrayed me. I thought we were going to be together forever but it didn't happen."

"That's terrible."

"But," he sighed. "I'm not going to worry about it anymore. I'm going to find someone else and get the hell away from her. Pardon my language."

"There are plenty of fish in the sea." I agreed.

"The problem is, when we get divorced, she's going to get half of my stuff. We never signed a prenup. I can't help but think that she intended this to begin with."

"Let's try not to jump to conclusions," I said. "It'll stress you out. You have to watch your blood pressure. It could spike up at any time like it did before."

"Yeah. That's true." He took a deep breath. "I don't know what love is. What's even real anymore? I feel like I invented a person who would marry me and be my wife. But in reality, that's all she was, an invention of my imagination."

An invention… Like Mr. Sam. Was she inventing a person too? Someone who could love her as much as she loved him? Was love even real? When it was over, was it still real? Or did breaking up invalidate the whole experience?

"I didn't do anything wrong," Miller continued. "How could she do that to me?"

"Don't be so hard on yourself," I tried to reassure him. "You didn't do anything you shouldn't have. Time will heal it. You'll see."

"You know what?"

"What?"

"I'm glad she's gone. She didn't leave me. I left her. Because she's a bitch. Pardon my language again."

When the session was over, my mind began to drift back to her insecurities about her new friend, Mr. Sam. I wanted to believe he would never hurt me. I wanted to think he cared more than that. I had to see him again. It was the only way she could chase away her relationship paranoias. But for now, she was working and she had to stay focused. That was the most important thing.

To my surprise, while talking to my patient, Richard, my sad boy patient walked in during my session with Miller. "Excuse me," I said to Richard. "I'm in the middle of speaking to this patient."

"Sorry," Richard said. "I just lost my wallet and I think it dropped during our session the other day."

"Oh, I see," I said. I stood up and checked under the chairs. There was in fact a brown leather wallet under the chair beside Miller. I grabbed it and handed it to Richard.

"Thank you," he said smiling. "I owe you one." He paused and asked, "Will you let me make it up to you and let me take you out to dinner?"

"I can't Richard. Like I said before, I still don't date my patients."

He shrugged. "Worth a shot." He glanced back at Miller on his way out. "Sorry for interrupting bro. Bye, Dr. Bell."

I shut the door behind him and turned back to my patient. "Now where were we?"

The day went on and finally, it was time to go home. I stopped at the bar I was regular at and drank two shots of vodka. Mr. Sam called and I picked up the phone, a little lightheaded from the drinks. "Hi Sam," she said enthusiastically.

"Princess!" he replied. "I wanna hang out. Where are you?"

"I'm at the bar. The one we met at."

"Oh okay, I 'll be there in a little bit."

Whatever. "Sure. See you soon."

He hung up and I ordered another drink. She was going to see Mr. Sam again and she was partly thrilled. This was even better than her crush in high school. More fun and more enchanting. I smiled to myself. Was he going to become her boyfriend? Like she had told him before, she had never been in a relationship before. She had never even been kissed. What kind of surprise was waiting for her now, Mr. Sam?

Mr. Sam arrived and sat next to me. "Did I get here too late to be vomited on?"

"Yeah basically," I joked.

He smiled at me. It was a strange smile he had never given me before. To be honest, it worried me.

"You look like you think I'm perfect," he said.

I looked at him. "Excuse me?"

"You might think I'm perfect Christina but I'm not. No one is perfect. I have my flaws too." He took a swig from the beer he had ordered.

"I'm not quite sure what you're getting at." He was such a weirdo sometimes.

"I'm like everyone else. Why don't you know that? My flaws are what make me who I am."

"What kind of flaws?" I asked finally, still wondering what the hell he was talking about. Was he drunk or something, because she was, and it would explain a lot?

"Like I lie," he said. "Somewhat compulsively. I lie a lot."

"Well, everyone has secrets." I shrugged.

"I suppose."

"Does that scare you away?"

"At this point," I said. "Nothing could scare me away."

"Well, we'll see what happens," he drank more beer. "I know I look like a good guy but I'm actually kind of a dick. You should probably get away from me while you still can."

"Where'd all this come from?"

"Just trying to protect you. I like you, you know. You're my friend."

Friend only? "I see. Well thank you but I don't need to be protected by anyone, and especially not you. You're a great guy and I like you too."

"I guess." He turned his face to me. "I didn't know this was a karaoke bar," he said, gesturing to the customer singing in the front of the bar.

"Yeah I didn't come here to sing but it's fun to listen."

"You can do better than that," he complained. He stood up and went to the DJ booth. Then he came back. "I picked out a song for us to both sing. It's a duet."

"Oh no, I couldn't. I don't sing. I don't even hum in the shower."

He rolled his eyes. "Come on, it'll be fun."

"Sam I'm too shy."

"This will help you overcome that. Plus, I'll be singing too."

"Ugh, fine," I said.

Three songs later our song came on and it was our turn to sing. Mr. Sam grabbed my hand and pulled me to the front. The song came on, a duet called Loving you. And I sang as loud as possible and completely off-key. Mr. Sam sang his line and I was surprised by how talented he was. He almost sounded like a real singer. When they were done, they headed back to their table and I said to him, "Wow. You're so good."

"I've done a lot of karaoke in my life," he shrugged.

"Even so you're good. Are you in a band or anything?"

"I had a garage band when I was sixteen. Just me and my best friends. I knew a Tom, a Darien, and a James back then. It was fun but that's where it ended."

I said, "Well you're good either way."

"Would you like me to put in another request?" He asked.

"Yes please."

"I'll try and find a new duet."

We sang three songs that night before heading off. Mr. Sam dropped me off at my apartment building. "Can I come in," he asked.

I shook my head. "I can't. I drank too much and I don't trust myself with you."

"A kiss then," he offered, puckering his lips. "I know you said you've never been kissed before."

"Not tonight," I said, feeling embarrassed she had told him that. He probably thought she was a loser. "No… I have to go," she said. She left him there like that and went into her apartment. She had never had so much fun in her entire life. This was her first time dabbling in karaoke and it had been quite enjoyable. Mr. Sam was a pleasure to be around. But she just needed to know him a little longer before

“A kiss then,” he offered, puckering his lips. “I know you said you’ve never been kissed before.”

“Not tonight,” I said, feeling embarrassed she had told him that. He probably thought she was a loser. “No… I have to go,” she said. She left him there like that and went into her apartment. She had never had so much fun in her entire life. This was her first time dabbling in karaoke and it was been quite enjoyable. Mr. Sam was a pleasure to be around. But she just needed to know him a little longer before she even considered affection with him.

Chapter 10

I'm here now
is what we say when it's too late
I always wanted to meet you
I think it's special like that
when you get what you wanted so perfectly
and the dreams take over
and we didn't lose our way.
Butterflies weave their cocoons
Dogs nurse their young
We're all wrapped in a natural circle of life
When we met,
Did you think my love for you was nature telling you what to do
Is that why you disappeared?

Mr. Sam called again the next morning. "Call off work," he insisted.

I had no idea what he was talking about. The Mr. Sam puzzle strikes again. And no matter how interesting of a puzzle he may be, she had obligations, unlike him, and she had to go to work. "I can't keep calling off work every day just because you get an idea in your head."

"Christina, this isn't just any idea. It's the best idea."

"Again?" I complained. " The best idea again? I'm not rich like you are. I can't just do whatever I want whenever I want. You're going to get me fired."

"Common, we're going to go skydiving," he beamed.

I pursed my lips together before I sputtered into uncontrollable laughter. This had to be a joke. If there is one thing I never do, did, or even allowed to cross my mind in my entire life it was skydiving. "No thank you," I laughed. "I mean, You want me to go skydiving. In the air. And then get saved by a backpack. Surely you must be joking. I would never do that. Don't you have any other ideas?"

"It's soooo fun. You'll love it. Common. You're wasting time. We should be in the air by now."

"Isn't it a little dangerous?" I pressed.

"It's perfectly safe. I've done it dozens of times." He reassured me.

"Is this a trick?"

"No. It's an invitation. And you're making way too big of a deal out of this."

I closed my eyes and moaned. This was crazy. She was crazy. Why did she keep talking to this guy? Was it because she liked him? Or was it because she liked the way he made her feel? Was this her story of how she opened up and became a more exciting person? She had no idea. "Fine," I muttered. "Let me call off of work." I felt like I had vomited the words up. It was official. She had lost her mind. Yes, she wanted to impress Mr. Sam but why skydiving? Couldn't he pick something easier, like fishing or something stupid like that?

Anyway, I called the manager of the building and he said it was fine for me to take one more sick day off. I hung up and called Mr. Sam back. "Okay," she breathed. "I got the day off and you can come get me." I was a lunatic. A stark raving mad lunatic.

"I knew you'd do the right thing," he said beaming.

"When are we leaving?"

"I'll be there in ten minutes," he said.

She hung up the phone and got dressed in jeans and a T-shirt. When she was ready, she waited outside for Mr. Sam to come and pick her up. As she waited, she couldn't help but wonder again if she had gone insane. It wasn't that she was afraid of heights, she was just worried that this would make her afraid of heights. What was she doing? I mean, did she just want to impress him? Or did she really reach a point in her life where she needed stuff like this to be happy? She had never considered herself much of a thrill seeker but as of the last few days, she was starting to think otherwise.

Mr. Sam pulled up and I got into his car. "Are you ready to go skydiving?" he asked. "Yeah." I paused. "I think I am."

We got to the air station and signed up. I was terrified. I don't even watch horror movies. Mr. Sam was built like a brick house and nothing phased him. Even though I had never considered myself a fragile woman, I was starting to feel like one around Mr. Sam. He was constantly better than me at something. I felt like if I ever tried to go somewhere new he would get there first. She felt like he was constantly telling her what to do and she wasn't sure how she should feel about that.

I know it sounds stupid. To just do whatever ridiculous thing Mr. Sam asked her to do. Maybe I am stupid. Maybe I should talk to a therapist myself. Was I really going to jump out of a plane? I couldn't believe it, but Mr. Sam was here and she had to believe it because this, like everything else on his usual itinerary, ended up happening anyway. We drove to the area where the sky diving would be taking place. I almost refused to get out of the car but did so after a few moments of bickering.

"Are you sure this is safe?" I asked, letting out a long breath of air. "You'll be fine. It's like a bucket list. You have to do this one time in your life."

"All right," I said as I got out of the car. "You win. What's the difference between dying like this or any other way? I mean we could die from anything really, sick, accidental, starvation." I couldn't think of any more examples so I cut it off there. "So how does this work, do we have to take classes or something."

"Yes. It's a six-week course." Good, they weren't jumping today. That would give her some time to think about it. She may even be able to talk him out of it. "I'm kind of scared," I admitted. "Is this necessary? I mean, do we have to do this? How much is this going to cost me anyway?" I was running out of excuses. "No worries. I'll pay," he said. He took me to the skydiving school's office and began to fill out some paperwork. When he was done he came back and told me we would need to be in class every Saturday for the next six weeks. Then they could get licensed and be able to jump solo or whatever it was he wanted.

When he was done, he had me sign something and then we were back in his car. "What do you want to do now?"

"I'm just worried about this skydiving thing. I'm not as brave as you are. I can't just do whatever I feel like whenever I feel like."

"I'll be jumping with you."

"I suppose. But even so…" I hesitated. "Never mind." I sighed, leaning back in my seat. He wasn't listening anyway. Kind of like how no one ever listened. Maybe the problem was her. What was she doing wrong? Why did she constantly get ignored by everyone she ever felt confident enough to speak to? Sometimes it felt like if it weren't for her patients, no one would even know her name.

He dropped me off at my place and I went to my bed and laid down. She was exhausted and they hadn't even jumped yet.

I wondered, why I called off of work again for him. I promised myself it was something I would never do again. I loved my job and I wasn't going to lose it over a summer fling. I grabbed my phone and turned on a '70s music playlist. Mr. Sam was interested in me. That had to be it. And he wanted to spend time with me. That was a good thing, wasn't it?

Even so, my lack of relationship experience scared me. I wasn't used to the attention. I was afraid I was going to do the wrong thing and make him go away forever. Was that a normal fear? I wasn't sure. All I knew was that I wanted to be around him for just a little bit longer before he did the most likely thing of dumping her completely. But until that day came, she might as well try to enjoy every minute of it she had left.

I'm not afraid of love
The sun feels cold
Even at its brightest.

I think love could be like that too
Colder than ice
But necessary to see.

I went to work on Friday and called my first patient to my office. It was Richard, the guy who had left his wallet in my office. He was as handsome and tall as usual. "Richard," I began, "What can I help you with today? Is the medication working for you?"

"I don't know yet," he admitted. "I've been having nightmares."

"What kind of nightmares?" "I have nightmares that I'm in a car accident and it's all my fault because I had been drinking."

"At what point do you wake up?" I asked.

"Right when the car flips over and rolls down a bank into a river."

"That sounds scary."

"It is scary," he said. "It makes me afraid to go to sleep."

"This is upsetting," I agreed. "What do you do when you get these nightmares?"

"Nothing. I just go downstairs, grab a beer, and try to get drunk." "Is that wise?" I drank a lot too so I knew the feeling. Even so, I had to stay professional.

"Probably not but I don't know what else to do. My adult life has been a charm. But my childhood still irks me. It's like the memory of it is pulling me down and I can't get up. I want to forgive and forget but how can I? I'm not strong. My mother was strong and protective of me. I want to be like my mother, who was a constant positive influence on me."

"Where is your mother now," I asked.

"She passed away a couple of years ago."

Flashes of my past came flooding out of my mind. I didn't want to expose myself but I felt a kinship with Richard for even just that one moment. "Me too," I said.

"What?"

"I lost my mother and father in a boating accident while I was at home with a babysitter." I stopped talking in the middle, terrified that I had dropped my professional face for my personal one. For some reason, she had felt so comfortable with Richard, that she had blurted out her personal life for no reason at all.

"Go out with me," Richard said finally after a moment of silence. "Let me take you out on a date."

"I don't date my patients." "I guess that is the mature response. Are you sure I can't change your mind?"

I shook my head. "Sorry."

"Don't be sorry. I'm not." He smiled at me. "How did a woman so beautiful become a doctor? You must get that a lot."

"I don't," I said clearing my throat. "Let's get back on topic. The problem we're dealing with right now is your nightmares. Do you have anything else to tell me about them?"

"Sometimes there's someone else in the car with me when the car flips over. I look over and watch them die right before I wake up." "That's terrible. You must've felt awful. And the meds aren't helping with these nightmares?"

"I'm not sure." "Well, don't worry, we'll have you fixed up in no time." "You were able to tell me about your nightmares and that was the first step you made towards stopping these dreams and curing your depression."

She felt so bad for Richard. He had gone through a lot as well and she felt genuine concern for his feelings. She wasn't sure what made him so interesting to her but she felt like they had something like a patient-doctor relationship like in the movies.

We talked for a little bit longer before his session was over and I had my next patient come in.

It wasn't long before work was over and I could get home. I hurried to my car and drove to my apartment, I was just unlocking my door when Mr. Sam called. "Are you ready for our first skydiving class tomorrow?"

"Like I'm ready for a staph infection," I said.

"That's the spirit. This is going to be the funniest thing we ever did before."

"Did you even hear me?"

"We'll both be taking class together," he continued. "I don't have a skydiving license either. We can give each other moral support."

"I thought you said you jumped dozens of times and that's why it was safe?" I snapped. He was going to be the death of her, one way or another.

"So, I lied. Who cares. The point is we're going to make it true and jump together. I'm looking forward to it. I know for a fact once we're up there you won't regret it."

Great, she was going to jump out of a plane with a compulsive liar. "That's not very reassuring," I complained.

"Common, please?" he pressed. He was begging and kind of reminded of a dog. I felt resolution melting at the sound of his voice.

Oh, why the hell not? There was no point in arguing with him. Mr. Sam was a spoiled brat and he knew it. She wasn't good at saying no to him and agreeing with him made him talk a little less which was nice. "Fine," I said finally. He got me. He had me right where he wanted me and he got me.

"Great!" he exclaimed. "The class starts at noon. I'll pick you up at ten."

"Sure," she said again.

If only her mother could see her now. Dating a cool guy like Sam. Would her mother be proud of her decision to Skydive with a boyfriend, or would she tell me otherwise? I want to do right by my parents. I worked hard in school. I got a decent job. I had my own place. Maybe it was time to have fun now. Was that the right thing to do right now? She wasn't sure.

Chapter 11

I can fly higher than you
You're a joke
But when I fell from higher up
It just hurt more when I hit the ground
Maybe you were right
When you said we weren't meant for each other

Saturday came and Mr. Sam picked me up from my apartment to our first skydiving class. I was nervous but almost a little excited. The promise of something new and different had seduced me and I was ready to fly and die. Whichever came first.

The two of us went into the skydiving school and sat down next to each other in class. There were several people already seated as well even though we were about thirty minutes early.

Class started and I took out a notepad and pen from my purse in case we had to take notes. The class started with a look at Equipment. The teacher pulled out all the necessary pieces for skydiving and laid them out on the floor in front of the students. This was kind of fun, I thought to myself. Like college had been fun. She liked learning and this was learning at its best. I snapped out of my nostalgia and went back to paying attention. When the class was over, Mr. Sam drove me home. "That was pretty interesting, wasn't it?"

"Yes," I agreed, still kind of mad at him for making me go. They were officially one week closer to jumping out of an airplane and no matter how fun the classes were, nothing was going to change that and my terror of such.

When we got back to my place, he asked "May I come in?"

"For what?"

"Nothing special."

I pursed my lips together. "No. Not yet. Maybe someday. Just not today."

"Why won't you let me come over?" he asked.

"I don't think I trust myself to let you in."

"Isn't that all the more reason to invite me inside?"

I shook my head, failing to see the logic. "No," I replied flatly.

"Maybe another time then. I can wait."

"You'll wait for me?"

"Do I have a choice?"

I laughed. "I'll see you later, Sam."

I turned around and was heading to my apartment when a stray cat came over. It brushed past her ankles and purred. She looked down. How cute. It didn't seem to have a collar. Was it homeless? She kept walking and the cat followed her. It was black with white paws. I let it follow me to my apartment. Once they were inside her kitchen, I went to the refrigerator, poured some milk into a bowl, and set it on the floor. The cat lapped it up quickly, purring the entire time. I couldn't help but wonder if she should let him stay.

She petted the cat for a while before deciding she wanted to keep it. She called the apartment's main office and told them she had a new pet cat. They added a pet fee to her rent, costing her about fifty dollars more a month. Not too bad. When she was finished, she left her apartment and went to the pet supplies store to get the cat food and toys.

She finished shopping, came home, and named the cat Tuxedo. Set up a bowl for food and a bowl for water and she set up the litter box. She dropped a few mouse toys onto the floor and played with Tuxedo for a little while before taking a shower and heading to bed.

Chapter 12

I wanted to recognize you as a man
As a lover.
As a father
As a husband.
When I told you
The man I recognized was not the man I recognized anymore.

I was at work, eating lunch with another doctor named Sara. I was eating salad and she was eating a turkey sandwich. I told her about the skydiving and she gaped at me.

"I never once pictured you as an extreme sportswoman," she exclaimed. "Aren't you scared?"

I nodded. "I'm terrified but my friend, Sam, really wants to go. He's covering the costs and is putting the both of us through boot camp. Classes I guess. We have to pass an oral and written test after that too. Then we can get a license to jump on our own."

"That sounds exciting." I shrugged. "I guess."

"How did you meet Sam anyway?" she asked, pushing back curly red hair. She was about the same age as me and a little prettier.

"At the bar, I go to every night," I paused. "Used to go to every night, I mean. With Sam sucking up my energy I don't really have the time anymore."

"So Sam is just a friend or is he your boyfriend." I paused. "I don't really know."

"Not even that?"

"No."

"You two need to work on your communication skills," Sara said. "I could never do what you did and just hang out with some guy without even a single clue as to if we were dating or not."

"Should I ask him?" I asked.

"No. You never ask a boy anything like that. That's like spraying your relationship with a weed killer. You have to let him breathe or he'll die." "This is all so much for me," I said. "But you're probably right. I'll just go along with it and maybe he'll ask me out on his own."

"That's the spirit. Patience is a virtue, my love." She swallowed the rest of her sandwich and excused herself. After Sara was gone, I finished my salad and drank the rest of my cranberry iced tea. I tossed out the garbage and jumped when my phone rang. It was Mr. Sam, so I picked it up.

"Are you at work?" he asked.

"I'm finishing up my lunch break," she said. "Why?"

"Do you want to do something when you get off?" I was a little tired but I supposed one more date wouldn't kill her.

"Yeah, sure. Where do you want to go?" she asked.

"I want to meet at the bar where we met that night."

"Oh, okay," I replied enthusiastically. "I haven't been going. They must think I'm dead by now."

"Perfect. I'll meet you there."

They hung up the phone and I checked my watch. It wouldn't be long before her shift was over. She just had to get through this day and then she could see Mr. Sam again.

Two more patients later I was headed home. I dressed in a skirt with a belt and a white lacey shirt. She put on red lipstick and was out the door. When she got there, she climbed out of her car and went inside. It wasn't that busy probably because it was before nine. The real hardcore drinkers didn't usually show up till around eleven.

I waited for about fifteen minutes and spoke with Dave about how she was waiting for her date to show up before Mr. Sam appeared at the door. I nearly squealed out loud in delight. He had his hair combed back and his eyes glowed in the dark. Talk about making an entrance. She waved at him and he came to sit down beside her.

Dave smiled broadly, "I know who this is. You're the karaoke guy and the guy Christina threw up on." "That is how we met," Mr. Sam agreed.

"Aw, I'm just busting your chops. It's good to see you again. What can I get for you?"

"Anything." He paused. "Never mind. How about a beer."

"No problem." He grabbed a mug and filled it to the brim. "That'll be ten thousand dollars," Dave said, setting the beer in front of Mr. Sam. I chuckled and Mr. Sam said. "Do you take cash or card?"

"Aw, I'm just messing with you. On the contrary, drinks are on me." Dave said. "Seeing you two is just too charming. You see I have a daughter that is the same age as Christina and I see so much likeness between the two of them."

"That's what Dave is to me," Christina said to me. "Like a dad to me."

"That's good. I'm glad you have strong people in your life."

I laughed a little awkwardly. "Not as many as you'd think." I shook my head and changed the subject. "So anyway Dave," I said. "Sam and I are taking skydiving classes."

"Really?" he looked surprised. "I never pegged you for an extreme sports athlete."

"It's new but it's exciting. We're going to our second class this Saturday."

"Aren't you scared the parachute isn't going to come out right when you need it?"

"Yeah, maybe. But that's what the classes are for. You have to get a license and everything. So it should be safe." I downed a shot of whiskey.

"What's the worst that could happen," Dave agreed. "Well, I've got to say, I'm proud of you girl. You've grown up so much since you started coming here."

I smiled. "Thanks, Dave." She turned to look at Mr. Sam who was slugging back his beer.

When he was done with his drink, he began rattling off his adventure stories for the night. He described the deserts, the jungles, and the mountains, he had mastered, survived, conquered. He was full of life and I liked that. There was a part of me that wanted to spend the rest of my life with him and another part of me that never wanted to see him again. What was wrong with me?

Chapter 13

We fall in love.
We fall out of love.
I didn't want to say anything.

Maybe I wanted you to say it first.
But you're not that important to me

It was Saturday and Mr. Sam and I went back to the skydiving school for the second day of class. I glanced at Mr. Sam sitting beside me at his desk and thought to myself that he was the only real reason I was doing this stuff.

Today, the subject was how to position your body and all the general rules for controlling your parachute when descending and landing. It was kind of boring but she figured she better try and learn something so she didn't die on her first solo skydive.

The sun was bright outside. She had to keep from turning her stare to the windows and the terrific weather outside. She started daydreaming. It was like any other daydream. Like what if she won the lottery, how would she spend the million dollars? I imagined a castle with Mr. Sam and me. How they'd go horseback riding and watch the sunset together while laying in the grass of the courtyard.

The teacher in front of them passed out a booklet that they apparently needed for the exam they would have to pass to get licensed. I awoke from my daydream to take a booklet. It wasn't very thick. It wouldn't take her long to study and memorize it for the exam in four weeks.

When that was done and the class was over, Mr. Sam took her back home and asked if he could come in. She denied him, as usual, and he smiled and drove off.

I went back to my apartment and helped myself to a peanut butter and jelly sandwich on rye bread. She wasn't normally this hungry but she felt stressed out from constantly feeling like she was entertaining Mr. Sam. She couldn't keep up with him. He was just too… I don't know.

What was the difference between one eligible bachelor over the other? He looked good on paper. He was wealthy and from an established family. He was tall and handsome and fun. So what was keeping her from falling all the way in love with him? She would have to be insane to pass up a guy like Mr. Sam.

She looked at herself in the mirror of her apartment's bathroom. And that's why she was in fact, not going to pass up Mr. Sam. Because it was stupid and immature and there was no reason not to fall in love with him. She'd give it time. Little by little, she'd let him into her heart and then she would be able to bring down the walls that had protected me my entire life.

I went to work on Monday. I was on time and straightened out with no intention of being reckless with her job ever again. She was a therapist. She needed to act like one.

She flew through her patients that day. She was getting her groove back. She hadn't needed to make any medication adjustments and everyone had been surprisingly well behaved. It wasn't until Friday that I lost my balance and tripped over Richard. Metaphorically speaking and literally. "Sorry about that," I said, feeling embarrassed. I had tripped over Richard's foot and fallen on the floor. Richard took my hand and helped me up. "Sorry again," I said blushing. "I'm not usually that clumsy. Is your foot okay?"

"Yeah, no problem."

"Let's go to my office?"

He agreed and we went inside. "Now what seems to be the problem today?" My heart jumped but I'm pretty sure it was just my imagination. The spiked adrenaline from falling was making her heart malfunction. That was the most likely explanation. It was either that or she was starting to think of Richard as more than just a patient and that couldn't possibly be it.

He replied. "So I have this thing I do every Monday."

"What's that?"

"I go to this sports tavern and order the same thing every time. Mozzarella cheese sticks and a corn beef sandwich." "You never skip one sandwich?" I asked, almost interested on a personal level with what he had to say.

"Not even one. It makes me happy and I know the guys there. And I guess my point is that I'm scared everyone there hates me."

"Do they act like they hate you?"

"Not exactly."

"What makes you think they hate you?" I asked curiously.

"Well, it's just, you can look a man dead in the eye and a man will convince you, you're friends. But when something bad happens, you become a burden and they don't even call anymore." Richard continued. "I'm afraid of being lied to, you know. Misled into thinking I was relevant just to make my fall from Eden a bigger one. So it hurts, you know?"

"Eden?"

"Yes. I feel like there are two powers in the world. The truth for one. And the False for two. Or To put it simply, lies and honesty. You give someone a lie, maybe it came in the form of a beer or a compliment, but he doesn't love you, he's just trying to bring your guard down and weaken your system."

"That's a lot, Richard," I said seriously. "I have you down as chronically depressed, not paranoid schizophrenic. Why do you think that this system is even real for that matter? You're a nice guy and I'm sure everyone loves you and is happy to see you every Monday."

"That's a bailout answer," he complained. "I just want to know who I can trust."

"You can trust me," I insisted. "I'm your doctor. No one's judging you here and no one is judging you at that bar. Think about it. Have any of them ever even said one negative word to you." "Not that I know of. Not to my face maybe. But how would I know? No one talks to me there."

"So your issue is with the fact that you think they're ignoring you, not hating you," I concluded.

"What's the difference?"

"Shoot. Your session's almost over. I have someone coming in about three minutes. We're going to have to wrap this up."

"You didn't answer my question yet," he complained. "What's the difference?"

"One is bullying you, the other one is bullying them. They're allowed to think and like whoever they want to without being told they have to constantly entertain you. Life is not a circus, Richard."

“Sorry, I asked,” He muttered. He looked at her. “Date? Are you going to reject me again?”

“Yes Richard, because it’s the right thing to do. I can’t go on a date with you. Not like this.”

“That’s fine.” He said quietly. “Maybe next time.”

“Maybe.”

He left and my next patient came in. Strange how no matter what she did, whether right or wrong, Richard constantly stood out in her mind. Where was this emotion coming from and why was she feeling it now of all times?

Chapter 14

You promised me it was real
That we fit together like twin yolks in an egg
Then you disappeared.
I still don't know where you went.

That night I went to my usual bar and sat down in front of Dave. It wasn't that busy but busier than the day that she had met Sam there. "Where's your friend?" Dave asked.

"Oh, I don't know. He usually calls but he didn't today." "Are you fighting?" he asked, pouring her her usual drinks and placing them in front of her.

"I don't think so."

"Do you want to try calling him?"

"Nah. I think I'll just enjoy it. I need some peace and quiet too you know and Sam is really loud."

"I see," Dave smiled. He noted. "Did you lose weight? You look thinner to me."

"Did I?" I guess I haven't been eating well. Mr. Sam had me running around it was no wonder I was losing weight.

"Meet any new friends?" Dave asked.

"Just Sam."

"I know a good girl from Russia. She's from a place very close to where I am from. Her name is Victoria. She'd love to have a friend like you. Would you ever consider meeting her for a best friend date?"

"Sure. That sounds nice. I need girls to hang out with too. Thanks for thinking of me."

"I'll let her know you want to meet. Her English isn't so good but it's about heart, not talking so you shouldn't have any problems." He pulled out his cell phone and called his friend. When he was done, he said. "She'll be here in about a half hour."

"Oh, how nice," I said enthusiastically. This should be interesting. Just like meeting Mr. Sam.

Her life was getting more engrossing by the second.

Veronica arrived as promised about a half hour later and she gave me a big hug. "Oh, girlie I'm so happy to meet with you. Dave tells me you need a friend too." She sat down beside me and Dave brought her a drink.

"Christina is a doctor," he explained. "She's very bright, like you." "I'm a therapist," I agreed. "And you, what do you do." "I am a cook in a very prestigious restaurant. It pays me good."

"Veronica's been staying with me," Dave continued, "until she can get on her feet. Come to think of it, you live alone, don't you Christina."

I nodded, drinking my liquor. "Why do you ask?" "Maybe she can stay at your place for a few weeks, just until her husband can come get her. It wouldn't be for long." "My husband is a good man," Veronica said. "He's a doctor too. But war has turned him into the bad guy. That's why we flee to America, where it is safe. He will come for me soon with our children. I wait for him for now."

"Oh, I see," I replied. "That would be fine then. I would love for you to stay at my place until your husband can get here."

"For free?" she asked.

"Yes, for free," I agreed.

"Yay!" she cheered. She hugged me again. "Toast to my hero. I love her."

When we were finished at the bar, Veronica went back to Dave's to grab some of her things and I drove back to my apartment to clean up my guest room. It wasn't all the way vacuumed by the time Veronica arrived but the bed was neatly made and the closet and dressers were empty.

Veronica unpacked her things in the bedroom and thanked me again with a big hug. When she was done we went into the den and turned on a movie. It was a romantic comedy and they were both enjoying the movie.

During the commercial, Victoria asked, "Are you married? Where is your family."

"I don't really have one," I admitted. "I mostly grew up in an orphanage when my parents died."

"I'm sorry to hear that. No husband?" she pressed.

"No. Just me." She thought of Mr. Sam. "Well, I mean, I do have someone I'm kinda talking to now. I suppose I could say he's my boyfriend. We haven't really talked about it much. But he does call a lot, almost every day actually. And we go out a lot."

"If he's so good, why do you not marry him."

"Marriage," I murmured. "No. I think it's too soon for him and me to be considering marriage of all things." However, it did leave me to wonder, what did Mr. Sam think about marriage. What were his intentions with her? Was he aiming at forever or was he just having fun with her? She couldn't help but feel frustrated thinking that she would never know until he told her himself and who knew when that would be.

"I see," she nodded. The movie came back on and they watched it in silence. When the next commercial turned on, she said, "Why did you not find someone else."

"Well, I love him, I guess."

"I see," she said. They watched the rest of the movie, ate some pumpkin pie from my refrigerator, and then went their separate ways to bed. Having a roommate was a little spontaneous for her but she liked Veronica. She had a good heart and helping a girl in need wasn't all that bad. She went to sleep wondering about Mr. Sam and what kind of hijinks he would get her into next.

Chapter 15

Why is it that when I see you
I can't think of anyone else
I want to love you
But every time I try
You brush me off
Like fresh fallen snow on your jacket

It was Friday, and that meant one thing. Richard would be her first client. She wasn't quite sure why she had made that association but she had, so she might as well live with it. She sat in her office organizing his folder when he came in.

"Hello, Doctor,"

"Hello, Richard."

"Any good news?"

"I don't know if it's the medication or your advice but I haven't had a nightmare in a full week." He said quickly.

"Well good. We're making progress then." She checked her computer and skimmed through his medications. "From a scale of one to ten, ten being the worst. How sad do you feel?"

"Ten," he said. "Sometimes nine if I'm drinking. I'm also worried that I drink too much. I'm a pretty stupid drunk."

Ditto. "What do you mean?" I asked.

"When I drink, I start to say exactly what I'm thinking and it's embarrassing."

I chuckled despite myself. "I see. Well, alcohol is a depressant. So it can feel good for a second but make you sad later. How often do you drink?"

"Almost every night," he said.

"And about how many drinks do you consume in a night."

"I dunno," he mumbled. "Like ten beers or ten glasses of wine or something like that."

"I see," she said. "I think it might do you some good to cut back a little. Not all at once but little by little so you can give your liver a break. That's clearly way too much alcohol."

"I agree," he said.

We talked for a little longer and then it happened. The thing he kept doing. The thing that kept happening after every damned session.

"Would you like to go on a date?" he asked me innocently as if he had never asked before in his entire life.

"I told you no," I said patiently. "I'm not interested." "Maybe next time," he said.

It was the end of his session so I stood up, opened the door for him, and reminded him. "I'll see you next week. My secretary will write you in for scheduling." When I was done talking to him, I shut the door and sat at my desk. Why was he always asking her out? Was he joking? Was he trying to make her mad at him? What the hell was going on here?

And what if she said yes? What would happen then? They'd go on a date or two and then end up hating each other. Besides, she had Mr. Sam and she didn't want to lose what she had with him. He was much too important to her.

I went home when work was over and went into my apartment. Victoria was sitting on the couch watching television. She worked the night shifts so she was dressed in her cook uniform and apron, ready to leave at any time.

"Hello Victoria," I said.

"Oh you're home," she said. "How is your day?"

"Boring and confusing," I admitted.

"How so?"

"There's this guy there. One of my patients actually. He keeps asking me out and I keep telling him no."

"Why don't you say yes to him?" she asked.

"Because I have Sam. It would be cheating."

"What is the patient's name?"

"Richard."

"Is he cute?"

"He's very handsome. A really good-looking guy."

"Sounds like waste to me."

"You're married so you must know what it feels like to have to reject someone don't you?"

"I'm not a doctor that everyone hits on," she laughed. "This is a real disorder you suffer from."

"Disorder my butt," I mumbled. "I just don't get it. First I can't get a man no matter how I try and now suddenly, I get noticed finally and there are too many men hitting on me. How did this happen."

"Maybe you're sick," Victoria joked. "Go to a physical doctor. They will fix you."

"You're no help," I chuckled. I went to the kitchen and pulled out a container of cream cheese and a bag of bagels. I heated the bagel and added cream cheese on top. This was probably going to be her dinner since she was trying to lose weight. Also, she wasn't hungry lately so no point in eating out of habit alone.

Tuxedo brushed up against her leg while I was eating. I paused to pet him. He was so friendly. She was glad she had found him.

When she was done playing with Tuxedo, she ate the bagel and drank some orange juice. The liquid felt cool and soothing on her throat. She went into her room and shut the door. Then she pulled out the book she had been working on and laid in bed, ready to read for the next couple of hours before she fell asleep. The book was super interesting. It starred a psychic police detective who solved all the crimes in the area with his mind. Pretty good stuff. Books were my favorite pastime. If there was one thing she liked more than alcohol, it was reading… Unless she could have both which was good too.

She was about halfway through the book when her cell phone rang. She groaned, leaning over and seeing it was Mr. Sam. She held the phone, listening to it ring. For once, she didn't answer it. She needed some alone time. She'd call him in the morning. They had to go to Skydiving class together, after all.

Chapter 16

You're on my mind
I've had my eye on you
I want to tell you I love you
But if I do, you might want me too
And for my own sanity
I just can't connect with you in that way.
If I did, I might start to hate you.

I woke up to the sound of my phone ringing. Shoot she was late for a skydiving class. She jumped out of bed and answered her cell. "Hi, Sam." "Why didn't you pick up last night?" "I was busy. Sorry."

"Now we're running late. Hurry up and get out here. I'm in front of your apartment." "Coming," I said quickly. She hadn't been able to put the book down and had ended up reading the entire thing. She didn't fall asleep until past five in the morning. I dressed in jeans and a tank top and rushed outside. She saw Mr. Sam's car and hurried toward it. She climbed inside the passenger seat.

"Sorry I'm late," she said.

"What happened?"

"I spent all night reading and I lost track of time."

"What book could possibly be so interesting that you lose track of time."

"Don't you read?"

"Not really."

"Oh, well I do," I muttered.

They drove to the skydiving school and went inside. Today they were studying how to move your body into safe positions and landing patterns, so you could land safely once you were near the ground.

I pulled out my notepad and took notes while the instructor explained in immaculate detail, the art of skydiving. I was just starting to get into it when the instructor informed us that next week we would start the assisted jumps with their instructors. I was terrified. Was I actually going to go through with this? Classes, maybe. A test? Okay. A skydiving license I'm never going to use, fine. But why did the actual skydiving have to manifest physically? No way. I was backing out.

"Sam, can I talk to you?" she said, pulling him to the side after class.

"Sure, what's up?"

"I'm not feeling too secure about this skydiving thing. Do you think we could just say we did it and bail? I don't want to do this."

"Relax. I'll be there. The teachers will be there. You'll have a good time. I promise."

"No, Sam, you're not listening. I don't want to have a good time. I want to do something else other than jumping. I'm scared."

"I'll protect you," he smiled, putting his arms around her. "I promise. Nothing bad will happen." "Ugh," I said, giving up. "Never mind." The problem with Mr. Sam was that it was very difficult to talk to him. He was always right. He was always demanding something. And he always got what he wanted. She wasn't sure she could handle a guy like that.

They walked to his car and he drove her home. The ride felt long and she was annoyed the entire time. She even felt bold enough to turn his radio on and turn the music up all the way. When they got back to her place, he asked if he could come in. Since Victoria was there and they wouldn't be completely alone, she agreed.

We went up to my apartment and I let him in. "That's a lot of purple," he commented, seeing the interior of my living room.

"I like purple," I shrugged. "It's pretty."

Victoria was washing dishes in the kitchen. She turned around. "Christina, how are you?"

"I'm fine," she said. She tugged on Mr. Sam's arm. "This is the guy I told you about." "Oh yes, Sam was it?"

Mr. Sam nodded. "Yes."

"Victoria is staying with me for a little while. Just until her family gets to America," I continued.

"Oh, that sounds nice," Sam said.

I sat down on the couch and invited Sam and Victoria to join her. When they were all seated, she turned the television on and found a movie to watch. "I saw this movie when it came out in theaters," she said.

They watched the movie and another one that came after that. I ordered pizza delivery and when they got there, they sat and ate pizza together on the couch. I had ordered half pepperoni, and half pineapple pizza from a place I used to order from when I was in college and lived on my own. They ate the entire pie and finished off with glasses of wine.

I wasn't used to company but I was pretty pleased with my makeshift hosting.

When the party was over, Mr. Sam left and I went back to my room to take a nap. I was tired but at least I had tomorrow off, it being a Sunday and all. I slept for hours and dreamt she was playing basketball with Elvis.

When she woke up it was late at night. I decided to take a quick shower and brush my teeth. Then I went back to bed and pulled out my favorite book that I had read more than twice now and started to read it again. It was the story of a poor working girl who meets a sweet old woman and their friendship grows.

I read it slowly, absorbing the story and feeling like I was there too. I read the first few chapters before growing tired again. I was still full from pizza so I didn't need anything to eat. I decided to go back to sleep.

Sometimes, I think about my past and I get sad. Like Richard. I didn't tell anyone how sad I was growing up because I was worried they would think I was a loser and deserved it. I knew being happy wasn't everything but it was difficult being sad. I wanted to tell Richard that it would be okay because she would be there for him whenever he needed a caring ear. But maybe that was too personal. He was just a patient after all. So why did she think of him just now? Strange, huh?

Chapter 17

I wanted it to be you so badly
Did I try too hard?
I wanted to stand by you no matter what
Is that why I never saw you again?

I was going through my kitchen when I realized I was out of salad dressing and lettuce. I found Veronica in the living room on the couch and asked her if she wanted to go grocery shopping with me. She agreed and we left, jumping into my car and I drove us to the supermarket. We went inside and found a shopping cart. I took us straight to the fresh produce aisle and grabbed a head of lettuce.

"You're vegetarian," Victoria asked.

"Yes."

"I can't do it."

"Well, it's healthy and I prefer it," I said, finding a bag of baby carrots and adding it to my cart. "Is there anything you want?" I asked.

She pointed to a bag of apples and I added it to the cart. Then I found a bag of potatoes and picked them up as well.

"Why are you vegetarian," she asked. "Is it for the animals' rights?"

"A little," I said. "I stopped eating meat when I was fifteen. My classmate was a vegetarian and he would talk about how much he loved animals and couldn't bear to have them die for him. I had this huge crush on him so I became a vegetarian because I wanted to fit in. I guess I wanted to be more like him. He was my idol and I loved him."

"I see," Veronica said.

"I know, it's stupid," I murmured.

"No. It's okay. Love makes you do crazy things." I thought about Sam and the fact that she was literally weeks away from having a skydiving license and agreed with her.

"Did you ever do anything crazy for love?" I asked.

"Yes," she replied. "I get married."

We laughed and I felt a little closer to her now that we were starting to get to know each other. She was almost sad that Veronica would only be staying for a few months before her husband came to get her. I grabbed three avocados and put them into a plastic bag before dropping them into my cart.

"How'd you meet your husband?" I asked.

"We meet on the train. I dropped my keys and he picked them up for me. He handed them to me and I was in love. I gave him my number and he called me right away. It wasn't long before we were dating and then he proposed to me."

"That's so romantic," I said. "I'm jealous."

"Don't you have Sam?"

"Yes, I suppose," I said. "But Sam and I have nothing in common. I feel like I want to get to know him better but he won't open up to me. It's like he's constantly putting on a show. I can't tell when to take him seriously. And he's always talking me into doing things I don't want to do. But he's nice and I do like him. I guess I'm just scared of falling in love."

"Love is good. Sam is bad."

"Why do you say that?" I asked.

"I don't trust him. He has a dangerous look in his eyes."

"He seems nice."

"All men seem nice at first."

"Yes," I replied. "I suppose."

"It's okay. You'll learn." Veronica said. "You'll see the difference between good boy and bad boy when you get to be my age. I'm forty and I know more than you do about these things."

The difference between a good boy and I bad boy. I hadn't even thought about it. Was Mr. Sam a bad guy? He was so charming and nice to her. How could he be anything else but perfect?

I picked up a loaf of bread and dropped it into my cart.

Was Mr. Sam, not Mr. Right? She had no relationship experience and Mr. Sam was basically her first and only boyfriend ever. Was he bad for her? She had no idea about these things.

"When I was younger," Veronica began, "I met a boy like Sam. He had answers to every question and stories for every subject. He was strong and handsome and I thought I would like to be with him. We talked for months. Just as I was starting to like him he started getting mad at me about everything. We started arguing. Not once in a while but every day. Then he got violent and he started to hit me. I couldn't take it. I tried to salvage what was left from what I thought we had but it was no use. He abused me until I couldn't take it anymore. And I left him. It made me strong and now I know the difference between a good man and a bad man."

"That's awful," I said, "You must've been so traumatized."

"I was."

"But Sam's not like that," I argued. "Sam hasn't laid a hand on me. I told him I had never even kissed a man before and he has honored that fact and not made a single unwanted advance. I'm a virgin and he hasn't done anything wrong."

"Virgin is more dangerous. You have to be more careful."

"I suppose," I said. "I just can't believe you went through all that."

"It's far away in the past. I'm happy now. My husband is a good man and he takes care of me and our children."

"That's good," I replied. "You're very lucky."

I didn't take Veronica's warning too seriously because I considered myself a decent judge of character. Mr. Sam was a saint and would never hurt me. Somehow I knew that.

When we were done shopping, Veronica and I went to the cash register to pay for the groceries. I put everything on my debit card and when I was finished paying, we went out to my car. I dropped my groceries into the trunk. Got back in and the two of us headed back to my place.

"Thank you for listening to my story," Veronica said. "I don't mean to scare you from your boyfriend."

"Of course. You told me something private and important to you and I appreciate that. I'm sorry you had something so terrible happen to you." "I'm over it," Veronica said. "It's gone. I never see him again and I am glad. I'm very happy now and you, you are a good friend to me. Thank you for your kindness."

"Anytime," I said.

I wondered what Mr. Sam was doing right now. Why was Veronica so convinced he was the bad guy? Yes, Veronica had been hurt in the past, but that didn't mean Mr. Sam was a terrible person too. He had been a perfect gentleman… sort of. Hadn't he?

Chapter 18

He picked flowers for me
And I put them in a vase.

He said he loved me
So I threw the flowers away.

So I went on another date with Mr. Sam. We went to a festival with rides and fried food stands. He took me onto the Ferris wheel and we enjoyed the view of the entire fairgrounds from up high.

The night was going well so far. I was enjoying myself. My cell phone rang and it was Veronica. I didn't feel comfortable picking it up while on a ride so I let it go to voicemail. "Who was that?"

"My roommate." "Oh, Veronica?"

"Yes." "What does she want?"

"I don't know. I'd have to check my voicemail." I said.

"I'm not crazy about your new friend?"

"Oh really, why's that?"

"I think she might not like me. She was quiet every time I talked when I came over the other night."

"Well, she's been through a lot and she has trouble trusting people. Especially men," I replied.

"Why?"

I didn't mean to but while we were on the ride, I blurted out what Victoria had said to me. "The thing is Victoria doesn't think I should trust you," I said.

"Where'd that come from?"

"I don't know. We started talking about you and she said not to trust you because you were a bad guy."

"Bad to the bone." "I'm being serious."

"What do you want from me?"

"Are you? Are you the bad guy?"

"I'm tolerating this conversation, right now."

"Well?"

"Christina, you know me, I would never do anything to hurt you."

"She said her ex-boyfriend used to hit her when they argued. She said he was abusive all the way up until she left him."

"I would never hurt you, Christina. And I've never been in a fight in my entire life. I don't hit women or men or animals. I'm kind of a package."

I sighed. "I thought that too. I'm sorry I told you that. It was rude of me."

"If you ask me, Veronica isn't all the way there. I don't like her putting this in your head. It's not good for you."

"She's just concerned about me."

"No, she's brainwashing you into hating me."

When the ride was over, they got out of the Ferris wheel seat and walked to one of the food stands. "She's not brainwashing me," I muttered. I ordered french fries and pulled out my wallet.

"I got it," Sam said. "No, I can pay for it," I said, more sharply than I meant to. "I have money. I work and I can pay for myself."

"Now I can't even pay for your food."

"I don't need you to pay for my food." "That's it," Mr. Sam said.

"What?"

"I'm leaving."

"You're just going to leave me here?" I asked growing annoyed. "You drove us here. How am I going to get home."

"It's like you said. You can take care of yourself."

He stalked away and left me behind. I rolled my eyes into the back of my head. I finished paying for the fries and soda. While they were putting her order together, she called an Uber and ate her food while waiting for it to arrive.

When she got home, she went to her room and cried. Why did life have to be so complicated? Now Mr. Sam was mad at her and she didn't know what to do. Was she supposed to apologize? Should she have just let him pay for her food? What was she going to do if she never saw him again? She would be devastated. If this was what it felt like to be in a relationship, she wasn't sure she wanted it.

There was a knock on her bedroom door. "What is it?" she asked loudly.

"Can I come in?" Veronica asked from the other side.

"Yeah, sure."

The door opened and she came inside, sitting down on the edge of the bed. "Why are you crying?"

"Sam and I got into a fight."

"I knew it."

"I'm so sorry," I continued. "I blurted out what you said to me about your ex hurting you and he got mad at me when I asked him if he was like that too and then he left me at the festival."

"I knew it," Veronica said. "He is a bad guy."

"What should I do?"

"You should find someone else. I know a good Russian boy. He will treat you right. I'll introduce you to him."

I paused. Maybe that was what she needed. Mr. Sam may not be right for her but did that mean that someone else was? Should she take Veronica's help? "Yes," she said after thinking about it carefully. "I'd like that."

"Great! He is a very nice boy. He works as a doctor at the hospital my husband works at. His name is Demetri. He was married once but has no children. He is thirty-eight years old. I will get you his number from my husband."

"Okay," I agreed. Was it possible to find true love? Did it even exist? Maybe this friend of hers would be able to make her happy and end her loneliness.

Chapter 19

Shhhh
You'll wake up my boyfriend
He's asleep in our room
And he doesn't know we're having an affair

So a couple of days went by and Veronica kept her promise to let her meet Demetri. It was a dinner for three. Victoria cooked up a giant spaghetti meal for me, Demetri, and herself. We sat around my dining room table and I took a sip of wine. "So what do you do for a living?" he asked politely.

"I'm a full-time therapist," I replied. "Veronica tells me you work with her husband."

"Yes, he's a family doctor. I work in the ER."

"That sounds interesting." "I make it my mission in life to save as many lives as possible," he agreed. "And yes, it does get interesting." He smiled at me. His teeth were crooked but he had a nice face and his hair was cut very short but it looked good on him. She realized that she was on the rebound and had just gotten into a fight with Mr. Sam but she decided to take Demetri as seriously as possible. She needed the companionship and Demetri was kind and a decent conversationalist.

"Do you have any hobbies?" Demetri asked.

"Yes," I replied, clearing my throat. "I like to read."

"Oh good. What are some of your favorite books?"

"Around Town," I answered. "Simply You. The mystery behind your eyes."

"And they are all, romance novels?" he asked.

"Thrillers. I like psychological thrillers."

"Ah, I get it. You're a psychiatrist who likes psychological fiction. You make perfect sense," he said, laughing graciously. "I like that about you."

I smiled and ate my spaghetti. It was delicious. "So what do you do for fun?"

"I like to swim. I go swimming every week. Or more. I have a swimming pool at my place." "In Russia?" I asked.

"No, in America. I own two homes. One in Russia and one not so far from here in New York."

"Oh, you must travel a lot."

"Yes, I do. Mostly for work. Sometimes for leisure. You know, anything to make my day go by faster. I get bored. Ever since my wife left me I've been on my own for a while now."

When dinner was over, Demetri went home and Victoria asked her, " So what do you think? He's nice, no?"

"He was very charming," I agreed. I thought of Mr. Sam and my chest hurt for a moment. "But I think it's too soon for me."

"Will you have another date with him?"

I paused. That did sound like a good idea too. But Mr. Sam and her still had some unfinished business and until they had ended it officially, she felt uncomfortable with dating someone new. "Oh, sure," she agreed. "I'd like to see him again. He was very interesting to talk to."

"Wonderful!" Veronica exclaimed. "I'm so happy for you two. He will make a handsome husband."

My eyes widened. Husband, huh? That sounded more scary than the thought of talking to Mr. Sam again. Was marriage the point of all relationships? Was that the only reason we did anything? So that we could have a quiet married family with a predictable itinerary? I was starting to be more scared of the idea of a long-term relationship than ever before.

The next morning, Demitri called me. "Hey, how are you?"

"I'm good. Just getting ready for work."

"Oh sorry. Are you busy?"

"I can talk. It's not a big deal," I said, running a brush through my hair. "What's up?"

"Well, I just wanted to let you know that I really enjoyed our time together at dinner. Can I be presumptuous to say you enjoyed it as well?"

I smiled. He was funny and clever. She'd be crazy not to like him. "Yes. I did in fact."

"Can I meet you after work? For coffee maybe?"

I hesitated. It was all moving so fast. "Sure," she replied finally. "I'd like that."

We hung up and I went to work. I went through the usual patients, Frank and Mr. Zimmeron. A Casey and a Laura. Their stories intrigued me and helping them made me feel better about myself. I was kind of like Demetri. Saving as many lives as possible was important to me too.

When work was over, I met Demitri at Tony's coffee shop. He pulled a seat out for me, a perfect gentleman and I sat down. "Coffee?" he asked.

"Cream, no sugar," I replied.

He went and got the two steaming cups of joe and sat down again. She accepted the coffee and took a sip. Mmmm. "So I wanted to ask you, what are your views on marriage? I didn't want to ask in front of Veronica but now that we're alone, I'd really like to know what you think."

"Well, I believe marriage is forever," I said. "I want to marry my soulmate."

"I see. Do you have any kids?"

"No. Not right now," I said.

"Really? And you're twenty-nine?"

"Yes, no kids," said again, clearing my throat.

"And your views on sex before marriage?"

"I don't believe in sex before marriage," I admitted. "Is that okay with you?"

"Of course it is. Girls in the US are so loose. It's good to meet a woman with high standards."

"Oh good, I'm glad you think that way," I replied.

"I have to admit, I was married before."

"Veronica told me."

"And I still love her," he said.

I frowned. Where was this conversation going and why didn't she like it? "What are you getting at?" I asked.

"Well, I just wanted to come clean about it. I like you but I don't think it's going to work out. I have to fly back to Russia tomorrow and I didn't want to leave you guessing. I guess that's why I told you that."

Oh great. One date and he was already breaking up with me. She was such a loser. What was she supposed to say? Thank you for being honest. It was a pleasure. What did I do wrong?

"And it's not you," he said quickly. "It's my ex-wife. I love her so much and I want her back. You're a beautiful woman and I know you could do better."

"I see," I said, trying not to cry.

"Like this. I've already made you cry. You'll find your soulmate. I promise. It's just not me." He stood up. "Goodbye, Christina."

When he had left, I went back to my apartment. Victoria was watching television on the sofa. "Well, your friend broke up with me."

"What?" she exclaimed. "That's not true. Let me call him."

"He said he loves his ex-wife still and he's flying back to Russia tomorrow."

"Damn it, Demetri. I am so sorry. I had no idea he considered his feeling unavailable."

"Don't call him," I said. "I'm already embarrassed." He already rejected me and I didn't want to think about it anymore.

"Honey don't be embarrassed. I find you a new man. Just be patient. I will find someone for you." "No thank you," I mumbled. I went to my room and shut the door. Thank god for work. If it weren't for her job, she'd have nothing in life.

Chapter 20

Rejection is like beer
The more you drink it the fatter you get
Did I set myself up for failure
Or am I just drunk
Let me know if you'll be my designated driver
I don't trust myself to drive

The next morning, I was in my office, determined to forget about being rejected by both Mr. Sam and Demetri. Richard came in and was a breath of fresh air.

"Hello doctor," he said. "How are you?"

"Wonderful," I lied. "And you. How are you?" "Well, I've seen better days."

"Are you still having nightmares?"

"I had two." "With the car flipping over?"

"No. This time there was an accident and my house burned down."

I asked, eyes widening. "In this dream, was anybody in the house?"

"Yeah," he replied. "Me mostly."

"Did it hurt?"

"Well I gagged and coughed from the smoke but the fire wasn't hot and I woke up before anything else could happen."

"Twice?" "Yes, I've had the dream twice now." He hesitated. "What do you think it means?" he asked me.

"Mmm, memories from your past, perhaps.? The house was your prison. Now there's no more house and no more prison." "You think the fire saved me from the house." "Yes, that's what I think."

There was a moment of silence before he asked, "Doctor, how do I become the man I want to be."

"What do you mean?"

"I want to be an honest, caring, and considerate person. I want to respect every culture. I want to save the homeless. I want to… be one of those rescuers who travel from country to country giving out food, water, and clothes to the needy. I feel like I keep wanting to do these things and then I don't because I get scared or discouraged. Maybe I'm not good enough to be me."

"Don't say things like that," I said. "That's a beautiful dream to want to help others. That's why I became a doctor, so I could help out wonderful patients like yourself."

"Really?"

"Really," I replied. "Do you feel any happier lately? Even just a little."

"Well, the medication is making me a little happier but that scares me too. Shouldn't I' actually be happy? Is medicine the best way to cure my depression?"

"Being sad is optional thanks to your medicine. Never be afraid of being happy even if it is with the help of medication."

"Afraid?"

"Yes, I'm worried you're afraid to be happy and that's something to be concerned about. I can give you advice and pills but in the end, it's up to you to decide what makes you happy and what doesn't."

"Doctor," he said.

"What is it, Richard?" I asked.

"Go on a date with me."

"I can't," I said, thinking of Demetri and Mr. Sam. "You'll just hate me later."

"I could never hate you. Can't you tell I like you? I really like you. These sessions have meant the world to me."

I shook my head. "I don't date my patients. That's the way it has to be. I have to stay professional. If I even consider a personal relationship with you, you'll go away like everyone else in my life."

"So you won't even give me a chance?"

"I refuse to lose you. Don't you see? If we keep our relationship professional we can see each other every week forever. If we fall in love, it'll just end in heartbreak and we'll never see each other again. I don't want to lose what we have right now."

"That was a lot," he admitted.

"That's how I feel about that."

"Well what about my feelings?" he asked. "Why am I alone when the only person I care about refuses to see me outside of her work? Did it ever occur to you that you're the one making me suffer? If anything, the source of my depression is from you rejecting me every week."

"And I will," I replied haughtily. "You can ask me all you want for a date and I'll say the same thing. No Richard. I'm not going to go on a date with you."

"Is it because you think I'm crazy?" he asked

"I don't think you're crazy."

"Is it because you think I'm ugly?"

"Richard you and I both know you're very attractive."

"Then why won't you be with me."

"Our session is over," I said gently. "You have to go now, Richard."

He stood up and shook his head. "Women. The things I do for a fucking date." He left and I let my next patient in, wondering if I had done the right thing or not.

I loved Richard enough to stay away from him. Why wasn't that good enough? Why did men keep telling her what to do? She'd rather be single forever than have to be told what to do by men for all eternity. It just didn't make any sense. Why couldn't they just leave her alone?

I went home, my heart heavy and confused. Richard had that effect on her. She felt bad for rejecting him constantly but if he would just stop asking her, it wouldn't happen. Why was he like this?

My phone rang. It was Mr. Sam. Great. I held my breath and picked up. Letting myself exhale slowly I asked. "What?"

"You're mad at me."

"What's your point?"

"I'm sorry I abandoned you at the festival. I shouldn't have done that. I was just so mad. I feel like Veronica tells you something crazy and then I have to hear about it." He paused. "Did you get home okay?"

"Yes, I ordered an Uber to pick me up."

"Oh good."

"Why did you call me?" she asked finally.

“I wanted to apologize and make sure we’re still on to go to skydiving class together tomorrow.” He said. “Please don’t be mad at me. I hate stuff like that. It’s so boring.”

I felt a little better now that Mr. Sam had called. She asked, “Are you still mad at me?”

“Not one bit,” he said.

I breathed a sigh of relief. “Well, that’s good. I do want to go tomorrow.”

“So we’re still on?”

I thought about the fact that the next class would have actual jumps and I closed my eyes before replying “Yes, you can come get me.”

“Great. You won’t regret it. Sorry again for making you upset. I’ll see you tomorrow.” They hung up and Christina smiled to herself. She was glad that she and Mr. Sam weren’t fighting anymore. Even though the idea of jumping out of the plane tomorrow terrified her, she was still happy that they would get to spend more time together. Everything was better now so she ate her dinner and went to sleep early, prepared to die the next day from skydiving.

Chapter 21

I saw your number on my phone
I wanted to pick up

When I did
You broke up with me

From then on, I never answer my phone unless it's my mom.

The next morning I got into Mr. Sam's car and we went to the skydiving school. They went over basic safety protocols and what to do in an emergency. Then we were supposed to head to the office to log in their jumps.

Mr. Sam took my hand and took me to the skydiving office. We filled out some paperwork and it wasn't long before we were in an airplane high in the air, our diving backpacks strapped to our bodies. I was so freaked out. I didn't want to do it now. Cold feet. Then I looked at Mr. Sam and he looked so serious and happy I just couldn't bail on him. I thought to myself that this was kind of like the nightmare I had when I was five. I jumped off the top of a building hoping to fly but my wings fell off and I landed on the ground. It didn't hurt but it did scare me when I woke up.

We were hooked to our trainers and we stood at the edge of the plane just to the precipice of space where we would be leaping out of. We all jumped at the same time. I looked around. Everything was spinning and twisting and I couldn't understand who in the hell thought this was fun but either way, my trainer pulled the cord and my parachute flew out. Apparently, there's a backup parachute we're supposed to know about but I didn't need it. I looked around for Mr. Sam and saw he was way below me. His parachute came flying out a moment later and we both fell to the ground. I felt like I was falling from heaven. The sky was so clear and beautiful and blue.

When I finally landed, I sat down to calm my dizziness and most of all, sat down so I could cry. I felt the tears coming. It wasn't long before I was sobbing. Mr. Sam came straight over the second he landed on the ground. "Are you hurt?"

"No," I replied, still crying. "I'm just so… Just sooo… I'm happy."

"Oh good. Hope it wasn't too scary."

"No. It was perfect. Thank you."

I continued to sob and Mr. Sam sat down right next to me and put his arm around me. "Shhh," he soothed. "It'll be okay. We're okay here."

I feel like a bird out of its cage. I was meant to fly. I was meant for many other things too perhaps. But I had been caged in for so long that I now feared my natural habitat. Like freeing a

killer whale into the ocean. Would I know what to do if that were me? Did that even make me happy anymore? I cried harder and thought about how nice it felt to be held by Mr. Sam. If he was starting to love me or hate me or whatever it was he wanted from me, she hoped he'd make his intentions clear soon.

We cleared ten jumps that day. It was fantastic. The falling. The air. The beautiful sky. It felt like she was dying a little every time she jumped. We had to clear twenty-five jumps to get licensed. I couldn't believe what I had already done. It was amazing.

When they were finishing the last jump, I closed my eyes the entire fall. If it wouldn't have been for the trainer, I may never have released my own parachute. When we landed on the ground, I met up with Mr. Sam and we embraced tightly.

"I'm so proud of you," he said.

"Thank you." I breathed. They were done for the day and my adrenaline was pumping throughout my body. I couldn't believe I had actually gone through with it. Mr. Sam was the greatest thing that had ever happened to her and she knew that now.

When they were done, they headed back to her place. During the car ride, I admitted to Mr. Sam about my date with Demetri. "I have a confession to make," I said.

"Oh no," Mr. Sam groaned. "What did you do?"

"When we got into that fight, Veronica got worried about me and introduced me to her friend Demetri."

"And you went along with that?"

"Yes," I added. "It was just dinner at my place. Veronica was there too. She cooked for us."

"Did you think I'd never come back for you?" he asked.

I nodded quietly. "yes. I thought I'd never see you again."

"You can't get rid of me that easily."

"Really?"

"Yeah. So what happened? Are you guys dating?"

"No. He broke it off the next day. Something about soulmates and how I had to meet mine."

"I hate to say I'm glad he rejected you but I am."

"So anyway, he went back to Russia so I'm not going to be seeing him again."

When we got back to my apartment building, Mr. Sam came inside with me. When we got in, the television was on and Victoria was in her room, the door cracked open. She was on the phone. "Great, Victoria's here," Sam muttered. "That woman has it in for me."

As if she heard her name, Victoria came out of her bedroom and looked at the two of them in surprise. "What's this? I thought we agreed no Sam," she snapped.

"What's your problem, lady," Mr. Sam demanded.

"You are my problem. You are not good for her. You should go."

"It's fine," I said quickly. "I invited him up." Veronica frowned. "Fine. Do anything you want." She went back to her room and shut the door.

"What the hell is that woman's problem," Mr. Sam complained. "I don't like drama. Especially female drama." "There's no drama," I reassured him. "Let's just watch tv."

They sat down and I offered Mr. Sam something to drink. "Wine okay?"

"Yeah, sure."

"White or red."

"Red wine will be fine."

I brought out the bottle and poured the two of us a glass before setting the rest of the bottle on the wooden coffee table. We watched television for a little while before he excused himself, telling me had some things he had to do before the night was over. He left and I felt lonely again. I was glad we weren't fighting anymore and wished he could stay longer.

I wanted someone I could love forever. I don't know why I keep trying so hard. Love should be easy. Love with Mr. Sam was complicated and sometimes annoying. I sighed. I was a mess. I might as well just enjoy what I had for now and see where it took me.

Chapter 22

Even when I'm happy
I frown cause I'm a bitch
Even when you're around
I let my lovers in
I wanted to be with you only
And someday
When I'm gone
And you're gone
I'll ask to be buried beside you
Because it's the closest you'll let me get to you.

Mr. Sam and I went on a date. We were spending so much time together I couldn't help but think that maybe I was falling in love. He took us to a bar I had never been to before and we took a seat. It wasn't very fancy but it seemed cozy, with wooden booths and a lot of windows.

"So how did you feel about our first-day skydiving?" he asked.

"It was amazing," I agreed. "You were right. I don't think I've ever had that much fun before in my life."

"So you're glad we did it?" he asked.

"Yes, I'm glad," she smiled. He brought out the excitement in her. She was positive about that. If it weren't for Mr. Sam, she'd be bored and alone. She didn't care what Veronica said, Mr. Sam was good for her.

"You are just too cute," Mr. Sam said, cocking his head to the side. "What are you doing right?"

I wasn't sure if he was joking or being serious so I just laughed and took a sip from the drink I had ordered. Mr. Sam was so confusing.

I thought about all the times in my life when I had felt disappointed or rejected. I was always such a quiet girl. Mr. Sam had a way of bringing me out of my shell. Were we going to be together forever? I wish I could see the future and know what I was in for. Anything was possible, really. Anything.

"How was work today?" he asked me.

I replied. "Just the usual. I talked to my patients and helped them sort out their lives. I guess that pretty much simplifies it."

"Your job sounds boring," he complained.

"Why do you say that?" I asked. "I like it."

"Why?"

"I like helping people."

"You talk to crazy people all day long. How is that a job?" I felt annoyed. "That's a lot coming from someone whose job is a figment of his imagination," I muttered.

"What was that?"

"Nothing. I said you seem to know a lot."

He smiled and drank from a mug of beer. "I do know what I'm talking about. You need to travel and see the world. Like me. Then you'll start to make sense. Right now you're just half a person. You need to do something challenging and dangerous and then you'll be a full person."

"Are you a full person?" I asked.

"More than that," he said. "I'm like two people."

"Two? How so?"

"It's pretty obvious, isn't it? I can do anything. Just give me a challenge and I can do it."

"I suppose," I said, taking another sip from my drink. He was so obnoxious. Was he even listening to her or was she just there too?

"What's your favorite thing about me?" Mr. Sam asked.

"Why?" "I just need to know you appreciate me. So, what is your favorite thing about me?"

Was this necessary? She was talking to a narcissist. "Your eyes," I said finally.

"Yes my eyes are very pretty," he agreed, sounding annoyed. "But I want to know what you think about the full package."

Ugh. He wasn't going to drop it until he was satisfied. "Your personality," I said finally.

"Okay, better," he said. "But you're still off." "Is there an answer to this question?"

“Yes, there is,” he replied.

“Can you just tell me the answer?” she asked.

“Obviously,” he said. “The answer is everything. You like everything about me.” “Oh of course,” I said, humoring him. “Everything.” She felt like she was talking to a five-year-old.

“But you knew that already,” continued, drinking his beer.

“Did I?” I asked.

“Yes,” he replied. He looked at me and flashed a smile. “Your life was so boring before you met me. This must be pretty exciting huh?” “Exciting?”

“Getting to hang out with me and all. Not everyone gets that opportunity if you know what I mean?”

“You’re definitely exciting,” I agreed, not sure whether to take him seriously or not. At least he was fun to talk to.

“Can I kiss you?” he asked. He was starting to sound drunk.

“No,” I said.

“Are you sure?”

He shrugged. “Your loss. Maybe next time.”

I nodded. At least he was being patient with me. I had very strict boundaries and I wasn’t ready to break them just yet.

He asked after a moment of silence, “ What’s up with the prude lifestyle? You have to learn to live a little.”

“I just want it to be special,” I replied.

He looked offended. “Hey babe, you’re looking at him. I am the definition of special.”

I had to keep from rolling my eyes. “Even so, I think I’d like to wait,” I replied.

“I think I’m done here,” he said, sounding annoyed. “You can get home on your own, can’t you?” I was shocked by the sudden hostility. “You’re leaving?” I asked.

“Yeah, I got things to do,” he muttered. He walked out of the bar and left me there alone. When he was gone I called an Uber and waited for it to get there. I paid the tab as I was waiting. Why did he have to get mad so easily? He was so close to being perfect. But then get so mad over the pettiest things.

I felt badly about how the night had turned out. I didn’t mean to upset him. If she didn’t kiss him, was he going to break up with her? She wasn’t sure. Her Uber arrived and sighing, she climbed in and let the driver take her home.

Chapter 23

I picked you from a bed of flowers
And put you in a vase
I let you stay until you are old and dried
You're still there to this day

Sam called to apologize to me, "I don't know what came over me. I think I drank too much. Are you mad at me?"

"No," I replied, secretly happy he had called. She didn't want one night to ruin her relationship with him.

"Sorry for leaving you at the bar," He continued. "Did you get home okay?"

"Yes, I got home fine," I said. He was really exhausting her. She didn't think there was enough energy in the world to keep up with this guy.

"So, we're good?" he asked me finally.

"Yeah, we're good," I said.

"I can't hang out today," he said, " because I have something I have to do. Do you have any plans tomorrow?"

Would he have cared if she did? But she didn't so she just went along with it, like she usually did with Mr. Sam. "I'm free after work," I replied. "What did you want to do?"

"I want to go bowling," he said. "You ever bowl before?"

"Yes," I replied. "I had a few friends in college that took me." She was exaggerating. She didn't want him to know that the one time she had gone bowling, she had gone alone.

"Oh great!" he said enthusiastically. "I'll pick you up tomorrow at seven."

"Okay," I said. It had been my fault really. I had pushed him and he had gotten angry. I told myself I wouldn't do it again.

"See you tomorrow," he said quickly before hanging up.

I was on my lunch break when he called. I was eating lunch with Sara again. "Who was that?" Sara asked.

"Just this guy I'm dating," I replied.

"What'd he want?" she asked.

"We got into a fight at the bar last night and he called to apologize. He wants to hang out tomorrow."

"That sounds a little dangerous," she said. "Doesn't it? He didn't hit you or anything, did he?"

"No, nothing like that," I sighed. "You see I'm waiting for marriage before I do anything. I want to be with a soulmate, you know? And I've been talking to him for weeks now and I don't think he wants to wait for me anymore."

"Just let him go. It's safer that way."

"I can't just break it up with him. I think I might like him."

"This guy. This Sam. He's the one you've waited for your whole life and you just can't break up with him?" she asked, almost condescendingly.

Why was everyone always trying to break them up? Couldn't they tell she liked him?

"What if he is?" I replied. "Why isn't that good enough."

"Just don't say I didn't warn you."

"You sound like my roommate Victoria. She said the same thing," I sighed. I wasn't sure what to do. Why couldn't they just trust her natural judgment? She could take care of herself. She always had.

Hadn't I?

When I got home from work I found Tuxedo on the couch with Victoria. I greeted her and she said, "Oh good. You home. How was work?"

"It was okay," I replied. "Nothing special."

"Are you still hanging out with loser Sam?"

"Yeah," I said petting Tuxedo. "We're going to go bowling tomorrow."

"I see," she said.

"We did get into a fight the other night," I admitted. I kind of just blurted it out. Which was a shame because now I was going to get lectured.

"What happened?"

"He's not happy about my decision to stay a virgin till marriage. I think he's tired of waiting for me?"

"You barely know him. How can he judge?" Victoria exclaimed. "Get away from him. As soon as possible."

"I know it sounds stupid but I just can't. I keep thinking something good will happen if I stay with him and I don't know if that good thing is ever going to happen. I worried I invented a caring person in my head but all I'm left with is a fantasy I created."

"That's why you can do better," Victoria insisted. She saw I was at a loss for words and said. "You heard me. I won't say another word about it. I hope your date goes well."

"Thank you," I said, breathing a sigh of relief. "That's all I wanted to hear." I went into my bedroom and dropped my purse on the ground. I was tired. I didn't want to be a drag when Mr. Sam came to pick me up for our date so I decided to shower and go to bed early.

Tuxedo snuck into my room just as I was getting into bed so I let her sit on my lap and pet her for a little while.

I thought about Mr. Sam and about my feelings for him. A part of me was afraid I was just interested in the excitement and another part of me questioned if I might be falling in love with him or not. Mr. Sam was a tremendous influence on me. He was always having fun and was to be around. But did that make him right for me? Was he my soulmate or just another temporary relationship that came and went like the wind at night?

I decided I missed him so I called his cell phone. He picked up, "Hello?"

"Hi Sam," I said.

"What's up? Something wrong?"

"I just wanted to apologize for the other night. I know you apologized already too but I just wanted to let you know that you mean a lot to me and I would never do anything to hurt your feelings."

"Hey," he said. "Don't worry about it. I shouldn't have left you there. We can make it up to each other tomorrow, okay?"

"Yes, okay," I replied, my hopes renewed. "I'll see you after work."

"Good night, princess," he said before hanging up.

I felt better after talking to him and maybe a little self-conscious as well. I couldn't help but wonder if I was good enough for him. Was he just putting up with me, or for that matter, was I just putting up with him?

I had no idea. Questions flooded my mind and I decided to leave them all unanswered for the time being. It didn't matter that I was doubtful of my relationship with Mr. Sam. The point was that I was happy right now. I think.

Chapter 24

I met you for the first time
After years of suspecting you existed
And knew I loved you
When you told me you weren't interested

Work dragged on and on that day. I was looking forward to another date with Mr. Sam and I was annoyed that my day felt like it was going in slow motion. I worked with all my patients as thoroughly as possible. I couldn't let my social life get in the way of my job but I have to admit, today was almost the exception. I really wanted to see Mr. Sam again and be reassured that he wasn't still mad at me.

When work was over, I nearly jumped at the sound of my cell phone. It was Mr. Sam. "Hi!" I said, after picking up quickly.

"Are you still at work?" he asked.

"Yes," I said. "I just got done. I'm heading home now."

"Okay, I'll be at your place in a half hour," he said.

I hesitated. That was about how long it took me to get home. I had kinda wanted to dress up a little if she had more time. Put some lipstick on or something. She was going to say something but decided not to, afraid it would start another fight. "Okay," I said finally. "See you there."

They arrived at her apartment at about the same time. I smoothed out a wrinkle in my jeans and straightened out my blouse.

"There she is," he smiled. "All ready for the ball. Jump in Cinderella." She laughed and climbed into his convertible. The top was down and the music was blaring. He got in as well and began driving us to the bowling alley.

When they got there, they rented shoes and were situated in lane 10. Other than my single attempt years ago, she didn't really know how to bowl. She picked a ball from the shelves and took it to the lane. Guess she was going first.

She rolled it and it went straight into the gutter. Okay, so she wasn't at a good start but they were going to be there for a while so she'd have a little time to redeem herself.

The ball came back to her from the retrieving machine and she rolled it again. It too went straight into the gutter.

"Not off to a great start, are we?" Mr. Sam joked. It was his turn now. He grabbed his own ball and rolled it. The ball hit the pins and they all went down. "Strike!!!" he exclaimed. "Perfect shot." He turned to her. "Your turn, loser."

Great. Now she was a loser. I picked my ball back up and rolled it again, tripping a little over myself as I did. I regained my balance and watched as my ball rolled slowly into the gutter. Then again. And again. She wasn't very good at this. She thought maybe they should've gone somewhere else instead.

Two rounds later, Mr. Sam said. "I thought you said you went bowling before," he frowned.

"Oh, well, I went once," I said, coughing out the words.

"Once," he repeated, with friends from college.

She was going to lie again but decided not to. "Alone," I corrected him.

"Huh," he said, grabbing his ball. He walked up to the lane, rolled his ball, and got another strike. I couldn't believe it. Were there magnets in his ball and the pins? How was he constantly doing so much better than her at everything? When he was done with his turn, he sat down beside her and grabbed her arm before she could get up and go for her turn to roll the ball. "Have you ever had any friends before?"

What kind of question was that? "A few."

"Are you lying again?" he said. "You can't outlie the master at lying. I don't think a single I've ever said to you was true."

"What's your point?"

"I want to know, have you ever had a friend before?"

I admitted. "I had one. In school."

"Do you still talk to her?"

I shook my head. "No. I think she went on and got married. As a matter of fact, I think she moved to another state and I don't know which one for sure."

"You need friends," he said matter-of-factly.

"You're my friend," I replied.

"You need more friends other than just me. I'm not your friend, Christina."

I felt upset. Where was he going with this? “What are you then?” I asked. “We’re never friends to you. It’s never a date. What do you want from me?”

“I want to get to know you and I’ll admit, I’m not happy with what I’ve seen.”

“Why do you keep hanging out with me then?”

“I dunno,” he shrugged. “You’re a little interesting. I’m going to give you a few more chances to impress me. If you can’t handle it, I’m going to disappear.”

I was so mad but what he had said to me, I thought I would cry. What was she doing here? Mr. Sam wasn’t even going to let her call him her friend. What were they to each other then? If he wanted to disappear, she wished he would just do it and leave her be.

Mr. Sam stood up. “Common, let’s get you home. I have stuff to do later tonight.” “What kind of stuff?” I asked

“Shhh,” he said, “it’s none of your business.” He paused. “I might call you tomorrow.”

“That’s fine,” I sighed. I felt tired and embarrassed by their conversation. Was this going to be the last time she ever saw Mr. Sam again? Would that be for the best?

He took me home and I went inside. I ran into Veronica. “How was it?” she asked.

“I don’t think he likes me,” I admitted, not feeling like talking about it. “He keeps getting mad at me,” Victoria said. “Listen to me. Even if he is a good man which I do not believe he is, he is not making you happy. Every time you go on a date, you come home upset.”

“That’s not true,” I argued, trying to think of a time she had come home happy. But even if Veronica was right, she didn’t want to think about it. “So long as he wants me, he has me,” I shrugged. “And if he wants to go, that’s fine too. I’m over it.” I went into my bedroom and closed the door. Tuxedo was on my bed and I leaned over to pet her.

My only real concern was work. Her job was extremely important to her and she was worried Mr. Sam may be affecting her concentration. It wasn’t easy being a therapist for so many patients. It was a difficult job, one that had always suited her just fine. If she didn’t get her private life straightened out, who knew what could happen?

Chapter 25

If you liked me any less
I'd be your enemy

Love is funny like that
That's why I never fell in love.

Richard, who was easily my favorite patient came into my office for his appointment. Thank goodness, someone who could calm her overactive nerves. Whatever the case, she was happy to see him.

"Good morning, Richard," I said. "How are you feeling today?"

"Just the usual complaints," he smiled at her. "I'm sorry to burden you."

"You're no burden. It's been a pleasure working with you."

He looked more comfortable. "Well, anyway, I feel fine today."

"Great. Anything exciting in your life." The word excited triggered a mental image of Mr. Sam. Which was the last thing she needed in her life. "Anything bothering you?" I asked quickly.

"Well, I went to the movie theater alone the other day. It was a little empowering. And the movie was interesting. It was kind of like a vacation away from being me for two hours."

"What did you do after that?" I asked.

"I went home, drank, and watched sports. You know, anything to keep my mind going."

"I see," she said. "And you've been taking your medication."

"Yes."

"Are you having any nightmares?"

"I had a few."

"The burning house or the car accident one?"

“They had three this week and they were completely different from my old nightmares.”

“Do you mind me asking what they were about?”

“I was talking to Mom and we were drinking out in the back patio and then it started to rain. It doesn’t just rain a little bit it rains a lot. And the yard begins to flood and soon we’re swimming. The water level just kept rising.”

“How did it end?”

“Just me swimming and looking for my mom and that’s it.”

What did you feel when you were having the dream? Were you scared?

“I wasn’t scared. I was sad. I kept thinking as it rained, these are my tears, these are my tears.”

“That’s very disturbing, Richard.”

“What do you think it means?” he asked me.

“I don’t know yet. I think the dream might symbolize your fear of failure. Your tears fill up your yard and keep you from doing anything else. Are you afraid of losing?” “All the time,” he said quickly. “I can’t tell you the number of times I’ve been afraid of failure. I’m my own worst enemy.”

“Yes, that is upsetting,” I agreed.

He turned to look at me and asked “You’ve been so helpful, doctor. Let me take you out for lunch this weekend?”

“I can’t,” I said. “You know how I feel about dating my patients.”

“Do you think you’ll ever change your mind?” he asked.

“I don’t know,” I replied. I had no intention of changing my mind. “We’ll see.”

Our session ended and I was almost sad to see him go. What was his infatuation with her? Why did he act like he liked her so much? Maybe it was a game to him. Maybe he was being serious. I wasn’t sure. But like clockwork every Friday morning, Richard would ask me out on a date. It was almost charming.

My phone rang and I picked it up. It was Mr. Sam. “We still on for skydiving class,” he asked.

I guess he did want to see me again, even after implying I was a loser with no friends, “Yeah, we’re still on,” I replied. If he wasn’t going to say anything about it, I wasn’t going to either. “Will you be here at the same time as usual?”

“Yes,” he said. “I’ll see you then.”

"Who was that?" a voice from behind asked. She looked and saw it was Richard.

"My boyfriend," I told him. "We have skydiving class tomorrow." "Skydiving! Wow," he smiled though he looked upset. Was he jealous? "I never pegged you for a skydiver."

"Well, my boyfriend is a little out there. He likes to do dangerous things and then bring me along with him. He's kind of like my fairy godmother."

"Is that why you keep rejecting me?" he asked. "You have someone already."

"Yes, that is one of the main reasons. And I do think the doctor and patient relationship we have is enough for me."

Richard said. "I suppose. Well, have fun on your date tomorrow. I guess I'll just head home." He left and I was left by myself again. My next patient came in, so I went back to work. She felt bad for hurting Richards's feelings but she had rejected him enough times for him to know she wasn't able to be with him right now.

Chapter 26

I'm so cold
even though it's warm outside.
What are you hiding from me
Mr. Sam
and do I even want to know?

The next two weeks were a blur. The only thing I remember is more skydiving jumps and then the test to get licensed. It all went so fast. So basically I got my skydiving license and that was the end of that.

I woke up the next morning and yawned loudly. I made myself some coffee and helped myself to fruit and cheese. I dressed, drove to work, and was finally in my element as I returned to my office. Richard was there in the waiting room, drinking from a bottle of spring water. "Oh good you're here," he beamed.

"Richard, your next appointment isn't for the next couple of days. Why are you here."

"Well, about that. You've been so helpful to me I was hoping to change my schedule from once a week to two or three times a week."

"Oh is that all," I said pointing him in the direction of my secretary. "Susan can help you out there. Let her know I said it was okay."

I went into my office and was surprised when Richard popped his head in through the doorway "Hey um, I wanted to ask you something."

"Of course. What is it?"

"Can I take you out for dinner sometime?"

"I told you no, Richard. I don't date my patients. I still don't date my patients."

"Well, why not?"

"Because I said so."

"Fine," he sighed. "I suppose I can take a hint." He gave a small wave. "See you in a couple of days."

He left and my confidence returned. She had no idea what she was doing right or wrong to be getting so much attention from guys lately but she figured she might as well go with it. It would fizzle out as most things in her life did and then that would be the end of that.

When she was off of work, Sam called. "I need your help," he said over the phone.

"With what?" I asked.

"My sister's wedding. It's tomorrow and I don't have anyone to go with. Do you have tomorrow off? It's a Saturday."

"Yes, I have the weekend off. I'll go with you." I said.

"Great. Do you have anything to wear?" he asked me.

"Not yet. I can stop at the mall on my way home," I told him.

"Awesome I'll go too and help you pick something out. My treat."

"Oh okay," I agreed. "I'll be there in about twenty minutes."

"Okay meet you in the food court."

I hurried to my car and began driving to the mall. Mr. Sam wanted me to meet his family. Was he getting serious with me? I wasn't completely sure but I had a feeling he was starting to like me as much as I liked him.

I arrived at the mall ten minutes late because of traffic and found Mr. Sam waiting for me in the food court by the chicken sandwich stand. "Sorry," I said, catching her breath. "I got here as fast as I could."

"Thanks. This is really important to my sister and that means it's important to me. Let's check out the dresses."

There were about three stores that carried formal gowns. We went to the first one. I searched the rack for a simple dress but only found nearly transparent gowns of sequins and glitter. "These are too much for me," I told him. "Let's try a different store."

They headed to the second store and she checked the racks there. Nothing in her size and everything was too neon colored for her. She had no idea what was in season and she didn't have a great sense of fashion to begin with so this was probably not as difficult to do as I was making it out to be, but I was having a hard time. Not to mention the fact that my failure as a dress shopper looked like it was stressing out Mr. Sam.

"Pick up anything," he insisted. "My sister doesn't care what you wear."

"No, you invited me so I'm going to do this thing right." We went to the third and final store that carried formal gowns and she was excited to see a simple black dress with long sleeves and a skirt that went down almost to her ankles. "Perfect," she said, showing him. "What do you think?"

"No way," he booed. "You look like you're going to a funeral."

"I thought you said your sister didn't care what I wear."

He replied. "I guess I did. Fine. I love it. Get it and let's go."

"Let me make sure it fits," I said. I went to the fitting room and asked for one of the empty stalls.

"This one," the fitting room staff member offered.

I tried the dress on in the fitting room. It was gorgeous on and fit like a glove. I came out to ask Mr. Sam what he thought of me in it but he was nowhere to be found. I finally saw him by the cash register and he motioned for me to join him as if he were in a hurry. He must want to buy the dress and go, I figured. I changed back into my clothes and came out with the dress.

"I thought you drowned in there. What took so long," he asked as I approached him by the cash register.

"Well, it fits," I told him.

"That's all I wanted to know." He paid for the dress and handed it to me. "I'll pick you up tomorrow at about ten in the morning."

I agreed and we headed out our separate ways to our cars.

I got home and showered before going to sleep. I had my alarm set to eight. I woke up to the sound of it beeping and I got up groggily. I dressed in the gown Mr. Sam had bought for me and put on a little mascara and hairspray. Then I waited for Mr. Sam to call me. He called at nine and told me he was already on his way. When he got to my place I hurried to his car and climbed inside.

"I just can't believe it," he said. "My little sister is finally getting married. I'm so happy for her."

"I'm flattered you thought of me," I said to him.

"I was in a real hard spot. Thanks for helping me out."

"Not a problem. I'm looking forward to seeing your sister at her wedding. This is very exciting."

We arrived at the church where the wedding was going to take place and it was beautiful. I didn't get a chance to meet with anyone else in the family because it was so crowded so I followed Mr. Sam around like a pet on a leash and we finally took our seats for the wedding ceremony. His sister came down the aisle and she was as pretty in her wedding dress as Mr. Sam was in his suit. When the vows were finished and exchanged we all headed back to Mr. Sam's parent's place for champagne and a light dinner. Mr. Sam led me to his parents' giant mansion and brought me to his mom and dad. Mr. Sam hadn't been exaggerating when he said that his parents were rich. "And you are?" his mother asked.

"This is the friend I told you about," Mr. Sam said quickly. "She's my skydiving buddy."

"Skydiving now," Mr. Sam's mother retorted. "Another dangerous hobby? I swear, what will it take to keep you alive? You're already 32 with no wife or kids. You'll be the death of me. I swear it."

"Now Now Pamela honey," his father interrupted. "Let's not make a big deal out of nothing. This is our little girl's big day and we're going to support her 100%." He looked at me and added. "Nice to meet you by the way." He grabbed Sam's mom's hand and led her away from us.

The wedding party ended and Mr. Sam brought me back home. "Thanks again for helping me out," he said.

"Of course. I mean, you'd do the same for me, wouldn't you?"

"Definitely." He smiled. "Bye, Christina."

I felt happy and refreshed. I went into my apartment and fell flat on my face in bed. I fell asleep instantly. There are going to be days like that you know. Where everything goes exactly right. I think this was one of those days. Even if it turns to sadness and I never see you again, was this love? If it only lasts for a day or two or three, is it still love? What do we do with the relationships that don't last forever?

Chapter 27

You smell like gasoline cologne
If I could
I'd wear you every night
and still want more
I brush your hair to the side
Is this love?
I kind of hope not

I was glad I had started hanging out with Mr. Sam. He was a pleasure to be around. But… even so, no matter how hard I tried, I could never seem to get him to look into my eyes. I thought maybe he was better looking than me and that was why but who knows,

That morning I went to my refrigerator and was irritated to see that I had no more milk for my coffee and no cheese and fruit for my breakfast. Sighing I grabbed my coat and went out to my car. It had started to rain hard, making the day even more annoying. I passed a woman on the street, soaking from the rain and in a flimsy raincoat. I stopped my car and offered her a ride and a towel.

"Are you sure?" she asked

"Yes, I'm positive. Get in. Hurry. You're so wet."

She grinned at me. "Thank you." The girl climbed into my car.

"Where do you need to go?" I asked.

"Just home," she said.

"Where's that at?"

"Here," She pulled a cell phone from her purse, dialed her address on the screen, and showed it to me.

"That's not too far from here," I said. "I can take you home."

"That's awesome, thank you."

We drove to her place and when we got there she invited me in and offered cookies and tea. I was flattered because I don't usually get invited to anything at all, Mr. Sam being a recent exception. Life really was getting better. So anyway I agreed to tea and went inside with her.

"Have a seat on the sofa," the girl offered her. A small dog then ran into the room yipping as loud as possible, jumping onto the couch with me. "Don't worry. He's harmless," the girl reassured her. "That's patches. His name that is. Its patches. Forgive my manners, I didn't give you my name. It's Tae. I'm 21 and I'm in college."

"Really, is that so?" I replied. "What do you study?"

"Psychology."

"Are you premed."

"Yes."

"Oh like me then."

"Are you in college too?" she asked.

"Oh no I've been finished with school for a couple of years now. I'm a licensed therapist."

"Neat. That's what I want to do too. Be a therapist."

"Yeah it was tough getting through school but it was worth it. It'll be worth it for you too. I'm Christina by the way."

"Nice to meet you."

"Nice to meet you too."

The two of us went on like that for the next hour or two before I decided to head out. It was the weekend so I didn't need to go to work but even so, I still needed milk and cheese from the supermarket.

"I have to run but it was a pleasure," I said to her.

"Oh in that case give me your phone."

I handed her my phone and she typed her phone number into it. "There. That's my cell. Call me anytime. I spend a lot of time in class and studying but I do enjoy a break every now and then."

"Sure of course," I replied as she handed my phone back to me.

I said goodbye once more before heading out to get my groceries.

Chapter 28

trust is made of glass
When it breaks
it's sharp and makes you bleed
I guess
I walked through miles of rain to get to you
I sailed every sea
Trudged every jungle
And when I found you finally
I was so disappointed

When Richard came into my office, he sat down and asked me "I'm still sad. I don't know what to do about it. Am I going to be this sad forever?"

"Of course not. You just need to give it more time. Talk to me. What do you think it is that is making you sad."

"I don't know. I quit drinking," he said sighing. "I guess I thought that would help but I don't think it is."

"Well, that could be a good thing." I asked, "Could it be problems with a spouse or kids."

"No," he replied. "Nothing like that. I'm not married and I don't have any kids."

"I see," I said.

He looked at me and gave me a crooked smile. "Do you want to have dinner with me tonight?"

"I can't. I don't date my patients. It's very important that we keep our relationship platonic if you ever want to get better from this depression you're suffering from."

"Fine. Put me in my place I suppose." He paused. "Thanks, doctor."

"You're welcome."

I finished my shift at five and went back home. I was just opening the door to my apartment when my cell rang. It was Mr. Sam. I answered. "Hello."

"Hey Christina," he said. "I need to ask you something."

"Sure. What is it?"

"How would you like to meet my girlfriend?"

"Your… girlfriend," I stammered.

"Yeah," he said. "I told her all about you. She'd be thrilled to finally get to meet you. We're going out for karaoke tonight. Would you like to join us?"

I thought I'd pass out from the unbearable shock. He had a girlfriend this whole time? What was wrong with her? To think she had thought they had something. She felt terrible. "Yeah of course," she said instead. "That sounds fun."

"Great, meet us at Great Fire Bar on Westlake. Are you familiar with it?"

"Yeah," I replied. "I'm familiar with it."

"Okay good. Meet you there at eight. Be fabulous. We're going to have a lot of fun. Hope you like singing with us. See you soon. Bye."

I hung up the phone and tucked it into my purse. I sat on the couch in my living room and began to cry. It was times like these that made you realize just when you thought you knew it all, you knew nothing at all. You were nothing but a blank sheet of paper collecting memories and thoughts. I hated myself right now and I didn't know how to feel better. He had a girlfriend and that was the reality. I didn't know what else to do so I got dressed and did my makeup and hair in preparation for the night ahead.

Tuxedo followed me around as if trying to cheer me up. I fed him and gave him some water.

I think I was wrong to think that love could come so easily. To think it would just appear and whisk me away in a matter of days. But it had been a pleasant dream. A dream I could remember and think to myself that it had been real to me and that I had learned so much from the experience. Nothing could take that away from me. My memories were forever and not even Mr. Sam could make that go away.

I avoided Veronica in the meantime. She was avoiding the traditional "I told you so," and she didn't feel like being lectured.

I arrived at the karaoke bar and saw Mr. Sam sitting with a beautiful blond in a tight red dress. They saw me and waved for me to come over and join them.

Mr. Sam said, "Christina! You're finally here. I was worried you wouldn't show up."

"Why wouldn't I?" I asked, trying to sound normal. She didn't want to cry but she thought she might. She felt embarrassed for even showing up.

Mr. Sam's girlfriend stood up beaming and gave her a giant hug. "Oh, it's so good to meet you. I've been telling Sam to meet new friends. I'm glad he finally took my advice."

"Yeah well he's a good friend," I agreed. I almost felt dizzy like I'd pass out but I found the strength to sit down and act normal. The bartender stopped by their table and I ordered a shot of whiskey and a dirty martini.

"Oh," his girlfriend said. "I wanted to thank you for taking my place at Sam's sister's wedding." She pulled out a small jewelry box and said. "This is for you. I wanted you to know how much that meant to me."

"I see." I forced a smile, took the jewelry box, and opened it, finding a silver necklace with a butterfly pendant hanging from it. "Wow thank you," I replied flatly. I wanted to be more gracious but I was kinda pissed about the Mr. Sam thing. Telling me he had a girlfriend out of nowhere was a stab to the gut. How could he do this to her? Didn't have any moral guilt for leading her on the way he had for the past several weeks.

"Do you like it?"

My attention was forced back to the necklace. "I love it. Thank you." My drinks came and I gulped them both down. It was like that too sometimes. That the saddest day you've ever had in your life was the closest thing you had to a real social life.

"Here," she said. "Let me put it on you." I handed her the necklace and she began to put it on me, connecting the clasp in the back. When she was finished I looked down and touched the pendant. "Live and learn," I mumbled.

"What was that?" she asked me.

"I said thank you for the gift. I love it so much."

"You're very welcome," she said brightly. "I'm glad you like it." She continued. "Sam told me he took you to see Jennifer?"

"Oh, the fortune teller. Yes, he did."

"She was a schoolmate of mine in jr high, believe it or not. Who knew she'd study the occult and do tarot for the rest of her life? But it makes her happy and I hear her husband works for a car insurance company. I think that's how they pay their bills." She looked at Mr. Sam. "Her husband does car insurance doesn't he honey? Or am I mistaken?"

"No, you're right. It's car insurance."

"Interesting."

He pointed at his girlfriend and whispered, "She doesn't work. Her parents are richer than mine."

"Stop that," his girlfriend insisted. "you're embarrassing me." She turned her attention back to Christina. "I'm Bethany by the way. I don't know if Sam told you yet or not,"

"He didn't," I mumbled.

"Oh well now you know. Sammy is going to sing a song with me when it's our turn. Will you be singing?"

"I don't know. I might," I said quietly. I ordered two more shots and downed them in single gulps.

The karaoke DJ addressed Sam and Bethany and they went onto the stage to sing a duet. They sounded terrible. I think. They were flat and offbeat, and their voices were too quiet and too loud at all the wrong times. Or maybe I was just in a bad mood. I thought to myself that I never should have come here.

When they were done singing, they sat back down and I stood up. "I have to go," I mumbled.

Mr. Sam frowned. "Where are you going?"

"I have to go," I said again. I left the bar and for some reason, Mr. Sam followed me. "What?" I demanded spinning around to face him.

"Why are you leaving?"

"Because of you!" I snapped. "The dinners. The skydiving. Did you do all this just to humiliate me today? What was the point of all that."

"I know, I know. So I messed up. I never meant to give you the wrong idea."

"Oh really. Then what did you think I was going to think? I thought. I thought," I sighed. "What did I think?"

"So I have a girlfriend. So what?" he said. "We can still be friends."

"No, Sam, we can't." I stalked back to my car and drove home. I wasn't going to let myself get upset. I wasn't going to cry. I couldn't give him that satisfaction. My hand wrapped around the necklace and yanked hard, ripping it off and I threw it out my car window. Fuck this. Forget it. I wasn't going to do it. Now now. Not ever. I wasn't going to let them get to me.

I went home, showered, and went to bed, staring up at the ceiling for hours before I fell asleep. I wouldn't give them the satisfaction of being sad.

Chapter 29

I didn't cry when he left.
He disappeared
I didn't cry when he came back
I just want my hoodie back

The next day I went to work with a heavy heart and bloodshot eyes. I was desperate. On my break I called Tae, the girl I had met a couple of days earlier who I had offered a ride.

"Tae, it's Christina." I was sobbing.

"Are you okay?" she asked, her voice concerned.

"No. I'm not," I cried into the phone. "I'm not okay."

"What happened?"

"I was hanging out with this guy. His name is Sam. And it turned out he had a girlfriend."

"He never told you?"

"No, he never said a thing."

"Honey, you'll be okay," she said. "You don't need jerks like that in your life anyway."

"I don't know."

"Look. Stop by my apartment when you get the chance. We'll have tea. Do you remember my address?"

"Yes," I said, wiping at my damp eyes.

"Come over whenever you feel like it."

"Thank you."

"Of Course. You're welcome."

I finished work. Just barely. I was still upset and no matter how much I tried to tell myself he wasn't worth it, I would think about our time together and I would think that I was in love with him. Love. To think I had thought it was love with Mr. Sam. I drove to Tae's and she let me inside.

"Christina," she said enthusiastically. "Did you find the place okay?"

I nodded a tissue in my hand. I dabbed at my damp eyes. "Thank you."

"Come in, come in," she said.

I went inside and sat down on her couch. She brought out hot tea and sat down as well.

"Now tell me everything," she said, sipping from her tea.

"I thought I was in love. He did everything right and he made me happy. And if I think about it, he even said he was a compulsive liar. But even then, I didn't think he was tricking me. Was he tricking me? Or was he really that heartless that he couldn't tell I was falling in love with him?"

"Like I told you over the phone," she said. "I don't think he was good for you. Consider this a positive thing, you know? He's not worth it. You'll meet someone else."

"Yeah maybe," I agreed.

"This is why I'm single," she continued. "I don't trust men. I never did and I never will." "Have you ever been in a steady relationship?" I asked her.

"In high school, I had a boyfriend but we broke up right before prom and that was basically the end of that. and you?"

"Not ever. I've never been with anyone before."

"That's more good if you ask me," Tae said.

"You think so?"

"Yeah definitely."

I sipped from the cup of tea she had given me. "I'm just stupid. A stupid dreamer."

"You're not stupid honey."

"Yes, I am."

"It'll be okay. I promise. It only hurts for one second and then you feel better forever."

"Thank you."

We talked for hours before I finally excused myself. I had to work in the morning and I wanted to go to sleep.

I was just about to fall asleep when my phone rang. It was Mr. Sam. I wasn't going to pick up but the fact of the matter was that he called three or four times in a row, driving me crazy and compelling me to answer my cell phone. "What?" I demanded.

"You're mad at me," he said.

"What do you care?"

"I wasn't trying to hurt you."

"You said you were single."

"I never said that," he corrected. "I said I wasn't married." He continued. "I also warned you that I'm a compulsive liar. You should listen when people tell you things. It would do you a world of good."

"I'm hanging up. I'm not going to sit here and be lectured by a sociopath."

"So now I'm a sociopath?"

"You tricked me," I snapped.

"Let me come over."

"What?" Surely he was joking.

"Why the hell would I let you come over? Can't you tell when someone is furious at you?"

"I just want to do what's right. My girlfriend and I are in an open relationship. It's when you are free to date anyone you want to even though you're in a relationship."

"I know what an open relationship is." Huh????

"Let me come over."

"My answer is still no."

"I want you to be my third girlfriend."

"You want me to be your third girlfriend. You have two already?"

"You said it. Not me," he replied.

"I… I don't even know what that is," I sighed. I wasn't sure whether I felt better or worse after hearing he was a polygamist so I was quiet before saying. "I don't know. Ask me tomorrow."

"Okay, get some sleep then princess. I'll call you in the morning. goodnight."

He hung up and I stared at my phone. He didn't want me to be his girlfriend, he wanted me to be one of his girlfriends. I was shocked. So he hadn't rejected her after all. But even so, could I really be someone's third girlfriend? It was such a foreign concept to me. Whatever happened to soulmates and true love and wanting to be with that one special person forever? I needed to think and sleep on it. Then I could figure out what to do about Mr. Sam. I closed my eyes and fell asleep.

Chapter 30

You said we were just dreaming
that life was long but kind
you reminded me to be free
and I think that's how I knew
we'd never be together
Don't judge
love
and when you're done
love again.

As promised, Mr. Sam called me the next morning. "Rise and shine," he said.

I glanced at my clock. It was about six in the morning and she usually didn't wake up till seven. "Yeah," she said groggily. "Hi."

"What do you want to do after work?"

"Are we hanging out after work?"

"Yes. I want you to meet Linda. She's my second girlfriend."

"From your open relationship," I said. "I get it. That's fine. I'll meet your second girlfriend. Is girlfriend number one going to be there too?"

"Not today," he replied. "She's going out with a Charles Donalds. He's completely aware of her open relationship status."

I muttered, "Unlike me."

"Hey, that kinda thing is personal. I don't just go around telling everyone everything about me and you and I had just met."

"Yeah, I suppose." I yawned. "So what are we doing today?"

"We're going out to dinner. My treat."

"Anything fancy."

"Not really. There's a pizza place I want to try out. I thought it'd be fun to bring the two of you along."

I said, "Oh okay, that sounds good."

"See you then?"

"Yes."

He hung up and I closed my eyes, laying back and yawning again. She couldn't believe it. Her first relationship in her entire life and she was now a polygamist. What would her parents, god rest their souls in heaven, say if they saw her now? I was tempted to pull back, give up, and shirk him off, but like I said at Tae's place, I'm stupid. And being in an open relationship with someone who had two other girlfriends already was pretty stupid of me. I sighed. Oh well. Let's see how this worked out.

I got to work and saw that my first patient was late and nowhere to be found. In light of that, I called Tae to update her on what had happened. "Tae!"

"Christina!" she exclaimed over the phone. "How are you? You sound so much better. Did you get a good night's sleep?"

"Not really," I admitted. "But something happened."

"What happened?"

"It turns out that Sam is in an open relationship. He wasn't tricking me after all. He intended on inviting me into his circle."

There was a moment of hesitation from Tae before she replied. "A what?"

"You know, when the people involved are allowed to do whatever they want with whoever they want."

"Like Polygamy."

"I think it is polygamy," I said.

"And this is a good thing because…." Tae trailed off.

"I don't know. I'm curious. I want to try everything with Sam. I think I'm in love with him."

"Honey, you're driving way too fast here. This is just another situation set up to make you cry again."

"It's fine," I insisted. "I might even start to like it. I want to try."

"You're right," she said.

"Right about what?"

"You should be allowed to do whatever you want. Just be careful. I don't want to see you get hurt again."

My patient entered the room and I said to Tae. "I have to go back to work. Thank you for listening."

"Anytime. Call me again if you need me. Maybe we can hang out and grab lunch or something."

"Okay." I hung up the phone and turned my attention to my patient. "So," I said to the patient. "Have a seat and let's begin."

Mr. Sam appeared at my apartment with girlfriend number two. She was just as pretty and bouncy as Girlfriend number one had been. I climbed into the backseat and Mr. Sam pulled out into the road. He blasted the music way up high like usual and all three of us danced as he drove. I was just getting into the song when we got to the pizza restaurant and parked. We went inside and sat together at a table in the back.

"So you guys wanna kiss or something?" Sam asked.

I couldn't tell if he was joking or not so I got annoyed.

"I don't mind," Linda said.

"Christina has never been kissed," he added. "We would be her first time."

"Really? I guess we'll have to make a good impression on her."

"No, I can't," I said quickly. "Maybe another time."

"Aww common it'll be fun."

"No, I can't. Sorry," I said, scared I was ruining the party.

"Well I'm not kissing her if she doesn't want to," Linda complained. "You're such a geek, Sam."

"What can I say? Thought it was worth a shot."

We ordered one large pepperoni pizza and when it came out, we ate the whole thing in about ten minutes. It was so good I even ate one of the pepperonis before discarding the rest. Mr. Sam was talking big again about his adventures and travels and how we should come along with him sometime.

I wanted to say that I was enjoying myself. I really do. But this aside from the pizza being delicious I wasn't thrilled at the idea of group dating. I asked him, "Am I your third girlfriend yet?"

"Yes."

"Then I'll try to do this for a little while. This is all kind of new to me so sorry if I seem naive."

"Of course not," Linda reassured her.

I felt curious for a moment. "Linda, how many guys are you dating?"

"Oh about four. You know not including Sam so four in a half."

"Why is Sam a half?"

"Because he's an idiot."

"Oh, I see." I laughed a little. I wasn't actually having that great of a time, to be honest. Mr. Sam was okay but it would take some getting used to be with a guy in an open relationship. I wondered how long I would be able to do this before I just snapped and told him to go away forever. I ordered a beer and drank it down quickly. What time was it anyway? When did the restaurant close? Was it just her or was it getting cold in here? The bill was paid by Mr. Sam and she wanted to leave.

'"Can we go?" I asked finally.

"Already?" he asked. "we just got here. I need another beer."

"Fine, after that, I really would like to go home."

"Why the rush Christina, are you okay?" Linda asked.

"Yeah, I'm fine. I'm just tired."

"Hope we weren't too much for you."

"No you were fine," she said quickly. "I just want to leave."

Leave it to me to ruin a good time.

"We can just go," Mr. Sam said, standing up and stretching. "It's not that big of a deal."

Relieved, she followed Mr. Sam and girlfriend number two to the convertible. She hadn't meant to stop the party, she just wasn't feeling well. All the new and exciting worlds Mr. Sam had introduced her to over the past couple of weeks, including this new-age dating thing he was doing with her was wearing her out. She wouldn't be surprised if she went crazy from fun hypersensitivity.

Mr. Sam got her back to her apartment and she went inside. She laid down on her couch and for the second time in history and fell asleep on it.

Chapter 31

I bite my lip as I look at you
You take my breath away
You were everyone and anyone to me
I need an inhaler

I went to work and Richard was there for his session. "Hello Richard," said. "How are you today?"

He sat down in front of my desk and said. "Same as before. I have this depressed feeling every time I wake up in the morning."

"Do you have it at work?"

"Yes."

"And what is it you do?" she asked.

"I'm an editor for a fashion magazine."

"Oh wow," I said, sincerely impressed. "That sounds glamorous."

"And it is," he agreed. "I'm just worried these feelings will get in the way of my work."

"These feelings, what do they make you think about when you have them."

"They make me feel like I can't stand being alive. I know it's dreary but I think about suicide constantly." He paused. "I have a confession to make."

"Go on."

He continued, "My dad was very abusive. He would hit my mom and me and he would get mad about everything. I used to be scared that I'd grow up and be like him."

"Richard," I said. "I think this is a very important point you've made. We may have discovered the reason for your depression."

"You think so?"

"Yes. Your father hurting you and your fear that you'll be like him is a very stressful and frightening memory."

He asked. "So what do I do?"

"We're going to get through this together. We just have to be patient and you'll be feeling better again in no time."

"Thank you," he said. He smiled at me, "Would you like to go out on a date tonight."

"Still no, Richard." I had to admit, the guy was persistent. It was almost cute in a way. "Why do you keep asking me that?"

He shrugged. "I guess I just like you. You make me feel like less of a screw-up."

"Well, I can't date you," I said. "But I can be your friend. If you ever need someone to talk to you can call me." She found a clean sheet of notebook paper and wrote down her cellphone number. "Here," she said, handing it to him.

"I can call you at this number?" he asked.

"Yes. Anytime you me."

"That means a lot to me, doctor."

"You mean a lot to me, Richard. I want you to get better as soon as possible."

"Okay."

When the meeting with Richard was over, I saw my next four patients. Then when work was over, I went home. I couldn't stop thinking about Richard and I felt proud of him for feeling like he could open up and talk to her about something as devastating as child abuse. I sat on my couch with a glass of wine and turned on my television. There wasn't much on but it was relaxing channel surfing.

When I got bored of that, I called Tae. "Hi!"

"Oh good, I was worried about you," Tae said.

"Why were you worried about me?" I asked.

"Well, I know you saw Sam again. How did the date go?"

"To begin with, it was a date with one of his girlfriends. I don't think it was much fun. Once we were finished eating I made him take me home. I'm just no good at this, you know? This open dating system may not be for me." She hesitated. "However he did say I was officially one of his girlfriends. Is that a compliment?"

"Christina, I'll be honest with you. How is being one of some guy's girlfriends a compliment? It's not normal. I'm not even sure that counts as a relationship?"

"I know," I agreed. "But I like him and I don't want to lose him. If this is the only way I can stay close to him, I think I'll do it."

"That's desperate."

"It's a fact," I said.

"Break up with him."

I smiled. "You sound like my roommate. And no. I can't. Not yet. I want to know more about him. At least for a little longer. Is that stupid?"

"Yes. It's very stupid."

"You're no fun," I joked.

"That's what you get for telling me about it," Tae joked back.

"I'm just going to give this a chance," I said. "That's all."

"I suppose." I could hear her sighing over the phone. "Just don't be mad at me when he breaks your heart again."

"Agreed," I said.

Chapter 32

When you're in love
he looks perfect
when you break up
and you realize it's better this way.
You say goodbye
and he doesn't even look sad
Maybe all relationships
are unrequited love
and we're just pursuing the shadow

Of someone who tolerates us only.
I just want him to pick me
Is that where I went wrong
sometimes love hurts
and if I wouldn't break an arm on purpose.
Why the hell did I do the love thing?
Maybe I'm stupid

Mr. Sam called me when I was finishing up at work. I was just about to leave my office when my phone rang. "Are you free this weekend?" He asked.

"I am. Why?"

"I want you to come to my parent's beach house. Bethany and Linda will be there too. We're going to party for two days."

I remembered my unpleasant experience at the pizza restaurant and karaoke and wasn't sure I felt like going. "This weekend?" I asked.

"Yeah. You coming?"

Despite this, I found myself agreeing to the invitation. "Sure. I'll go."

"Great!" he replied. "you won't regret it. We're going to have a lot of fun."

"Sounds good."

He hung up the phone and I immediately called Tae. She agreed to meet her at Tony's Coffee Shop. I drove straight there and found her already sitting in the back with a laptop and a cup of hot tea. "Hey Christina," Tae called, waving at her.

I joined her at the table. "You working on something?" I asked, noting the computer in front of her.

"Yeah, for school. It's just an essay but it's due tomorrow so I have to work on it."

"I see," I said. "So guess what happened?"

"Oh no, more about Sam the polygamist."

"I'm afraid so," I laughed.

"What is it?"

"He wants me to go to his beach house?"

"Alone?"

"With his other girlfriends. He wants us to all be there."

"What did you tell him?"

"I couldn't help it, I said yes."

"This sounds dangerous to me."

"How so?"

"I mean think about it?" she said. "Sam's obviously a very experimental person. And with three beautiful women there. There's probably going to be a lot of sex. Are you sure you want to go? Are you even safe?"

"I'm not a baby," I reassured her. "I can take care of myself."

"I'm not doubting that. I just think you should be careful."

"I'll be careful. Really, it's not a big deal."

"Plus doesn't seeing him with those girls make you jealous? I mean, If I were you, I wouldn't be able to do it. I would be mad the whole time."

"I do get a little jealous," I admitted. "I don't know why. At least I get to spend some more time with him. I think I'm falling in love and I don't think he feels the same. I don't think he understands me. It's like he can't even see me and I'm trying to get a hold of him and he won't answer."

"This is a bad idea," Tae said, shaking her head.

I took her hand. "Don't worry about me. Worry about your essay. It's due tomorrow, right?"

She smiled at me. "Right."

Chapter 33

I'm glad we met
but most of all
I'm glad we never saw each other again

The weekend came and Mr. Sam picked me up with Bethany and Linda already in the car. The beach house would be a four-hour drive. Mr. Sam and his girlfriends talked on and on about their adventures. None of them had jobs and I was beginning to get self-conscious. It must be nice having rich parents, I thought to myself. I couldn't even imagine it. Each of them was addicted to something. Bethany was addicted to drugs, Linda was addicted to gambling, and Mr. Sam was addicted to women.

"But what's your vice?" Linda asked, looking at me. "Christina what do you waste yourself with."

"Alcohol I guess," I replied. "I drink a lot. Like my dad before he…"

"Before he what?" she pressed.

"Died." I finished.

"Oh," she said frowning, settling back in her seat. " I see."

The four hours came and went and it wasn't long before we were parked in front of the beach house. It was very pretty, with lots of glass windows and a modern interior. The kitchen was stocked with liquor. The place basically had everything except for food.

"Looks like we're ordering out," Mr. Sam said. "What do you guys want?"

"Burritos," Bethany said.

"That sounds good. Burritos," Linda agreed.

"And you Christina," Mr. Sam asked. "What would you like."

"Burritos is fine," I said. "Vegetarian?"

"Okay, good. Then we're all thinking the same thing." He pulled out his cell phone and ordered.

Bethany grabbed Linda's hand and pulled her towards the den. "Let's explore," she said.

Linda nodded and I was left with Mr. Sam.

"Don't you want to go with the girls?" Mr. Sam asked me.

"Oh I didn't think I was invited," I replied lamely.

"Of course you were. We're all friends here."

"I suppose," I said.

"Or you can just hang out here with me?" he smiled.

"And do what exactly?" I asked

"Dance." He grabbed his cell phone, turned some jazzy music on, and then grabbed me by the waist.

He spun me and I laughed. This was actually kind of fun. "I've never danced with someone before," I admitted.

"Then allow me to be the first, madam," he said. He led the way, spinning me and we danced until the song was over.

Maybe coming here wasn't a mistake after all. Mr. Sam always managed to keep her entertained.

Chapter 34

I never said what I wanted
I never whispered what I needed
if you're so convinced you're better than me
then never call me again
I'm no longer interested in you

That night at the beach house, we sat on the sofas, ate burritos, and watched a movie. I had never seen the movie before but it had good reviews. Mr. Sam had Linda and Bethany laying on him and I lay alone on my couch. I felt a little left out but decided not to make a big deal out of it. I took a sip of cola and finished off my vegetarian burrito. When I was done I turned my attention back to the film. It was an action thriller called Spiderweb and it was pretty in-depth. She always liked these kinds of psychological thrillers. Psychology fascinated her and that was probably why she decided to become a psychiatrist herself.

Despite how interesting the movie was, she ended up falling asleep towards the end of it. A few hours later, I woke up to strange noises. I climbed off the couch and saw that it was dark and there was no one else around. The noise sounded again and she slowly headed towards it to investigate. It was coming from upstairs. She slowly snuck up the stairs and followed the noise to one of the bedrooms. The door was open a crack and as she got closer, she realized it was Mr. Sam and the girls having sex. Ew!!!

She pulled away quickly and headed back downstairs. They were having a threesome, right under the same roof as her. She felt embarrassed and appalled and kind of grossed out. She called Tae on her cell phone, curling herself up on the couch. "You were right, Tae."

"I told you."

"They're doing it right now. I am just completely embarrassed."

"Obviously," Tac continued. "What did you think a guy like that would do if he was alone with a bunch of young women."

"I mean do I just go to sleep and ignore them," I asked. "Do I join in and ask why I wasn't invited."

"I thought you were a virgin."

"I know, you're right. This is the kind of uninvited I need. I don't want to have sex here and I don't want to hang out with these stupid girls."

"You're jealous."

"A little."

"Well don't be. Just tell yourself you're not missing much." Tae giggled and so did I.

"I'm going back to sleep," I concluded. "I have a room upstairs but I think I'll stay down here for the night. Where it's safe," I joked.

"Good for you. Just remember three important things for your weekend out of town."

"What three things."

"No sex. No kissing. And no ice cream."

"Why no ice cream."

"Because it's an aphrodisiac. It leads to sex and kissing."

"If you say so," I agreed.

"So you're going back to sleep."

"Yeah, I think so."

"Goodnight then."

"Goodnight."

I woke up the next morning, feeling especially thirsty. I went to the kitchen and drank a glass of water from the tap. The coffee machine was already done making coffee so I poured some into a mug I had found in the cupboard. The strange noise from the night before echoed down the upstairs hallway and the staircase. She couldn't believe it. They were doing it again. Yuck.

She went into the den and sat down on the couch. Her cell phone rang and she picked it up.

"Hello?"

"Hi, Dr. It's me, Richard."

Oh, that's right. She had forgotten she had given him her number. "It's Christina, what can I do for you?"

"I had that dream again."

"Which dream," she asked.

"The dream that I'm drinking and then get into a car accident right afterward."

"You happened again?"

"Twice this week now. The accident is always the same. My car tips over and it falls down a gorge."

"That sounds frightening."

"It was. Well, It is. Every time I have it."

He paused. "Is something wrong?"

"With me?" I asked.

"Yeah, you don't sound happy. Here I am complaining about myself. Is there anything you want to talk to me about?"

"I'm fine," I said. The sounds from upstairs grew louder and more audibly sexual before I turned my attention back to Richard. "Like I said. Nothing is wrong."

"Are you sure?"

"Yes. Now tell me more about this dream."

"Uh I dunno," he continued. "I'm just worried it's related to being abused by my dad."

"I see. Yes, that is possible. Dreams tell us all kinds of things you know. Do you ever write down your dreams? Some people have dream journals where they hurry and write down the dream before they forget what happened in the dream."

"I might try that. Maybe if I do that I can remember the good dreams and not just the bad ones."

"That's the spirit," I replied.

The noise upstairs got louder and I was this close to telling them to shut up. "Can I call you back?" I asked.

"Yeah of course."

"Great, give me like ten minutes."

"Okay."

I hung up, went upstairs, changed into my swimsuit, and grabbed a beach towel. I went outside and laid the towel down on the sand. I laid down, using my purse as a pillow. The sun was high and felt great on her bare skin. She might as well tan while they infected the entire beach house with STDs She picked up her cell phone and called Richard back. "Sorry about that," she said. "I just had to come outside and get some air."

"Well, you sound better."

"Do I?"

"You do. Are you sure there's nothing wrong?"

She hesitated. "I don't know if I should be telling you things like that. You are a patient. It wouldn't be normal."

"I don't mind," he insisted.

I didn't know what to say. He was so kind to worry about her and wanted to go on dates and she was constantly rejecting him. I don't know what compelled me to open up but I started talking as if he had been best friends with her since elementary school. "This is the thing," she explained quickly. "I met this guy. I thought it was love. It turned out he had two other girlfriends. They're in this open relationship apparently and I can't stand it. I wanted to be with him but he doesn't even notice when I'm not there. I'm at his beach house this weekend and all he's done so far is have a threesome with his two other girlfriends. It's awful. I'm jealous, I don't feel loved, and I hate it."

"That's what you've been hiding from me this whole time," Richard said. "I knew something was bothering you. I could just tell."

"But enough about me, what about you and your dreams? Do you still want to talk about it?"

"I just want to be a good guy, you know. I want to be that guy that opens doors and takes a girl out and treats her like a queen. Then I think of my father and I think, why the hell did he do that to us? I don't understand what he was constantly mad about. If I end up like him. If I ever end like him…"

"If you ever end up like him what?" I asked gently.

"I can't be held responsible for what I'd do to myself."

"Do you feel suicidal?" asked, sincerely concerned.

"Is that the doctor in you asking that question or is it Christina that wants to know?"

"As a friend," I said. "A friend who cares."

"That really means a lot to me," Richard said.

We talked for another five hours before hanging up. I skipped breakfast and lunch before I realized how much time had gone by. Mostly because I was starving, I went back into the beach house and almost screamed out loud at the noises coming from the bedroom. What round were they on anyway? It was disturbing. There were empty food cartons all over the counter, making her think they had already eaten. I found a container of Alfredo with my name on it and ate it quickly. At least they were considerate enough to get her some food too while she was outside.

I ate my pasta, ignored the noise coming from upstairs, and thought about Richard. He was so sweet. Like candy without the diabetes. I wanted to let him know that no matter what, even if there was no one else, I would always be there for him, a friend he could talk to. I just wished I had told him that over the phone.

Why hadn't I?

Chapter 35

The future is all I have left
I don't think I did it right
If regret were a drug
I would light up every blunt in the country
I make mistakes
Mistakes of the past.

Because when you fall in love
an hour is like a second
and a day is like a dream
and I wouldn't let you have me
And that's why you're gone
Because you hate me
And I forgive you
repeat

Later that evening, Mr. Sam came down with both Bethany and Linda. They were all in bathrobe and their hair was wet meaning they probably all just took a shower together. I don't know. I don't care.

"Christina," Mr. Sam exclaimed. "Where the hell have you been?"

"Sunbathing."

"Alone?"

"I was on the phone."

"Oh okay. All's good. Did you eat the pasta I left for you?"

"I did."

"Wanna come upstairs. We're doing kinky stuff up there."

"I can't."

"Why'd' you even come if you don't want to play," Bethany asked, almost rudely.

Mr. Sam stared daggers at Bethany before saying. "She can do whatever she wants. That's why I invited her here."

"Whatever," she said. She turned around and went upstairs back to the bedroom.

"So you coming or aren't you?" Mr. Sam asked.

"I can't."

"I told you she wouldn't come." Linda said matter-of-factly.

Pursing his lips, he asked once more. "Last chance, Christina. What's it going to be."

"No," I said finally. "I'm not interested."

"Have it your way. If you want to be miserable and alone forever that's up to you. I'm going to do whatever I want, whenever I want to and if you can't be cool with that then I can't help you."

I felt my annoyance growing. "You know what, why'd you even invite me."

"I thought it would help you loosen up."

"I'm not loosened up."

"So it didn't work," he shrugged. "Big deal. Just enjoy the rest of our weekend here alone in the dark eating cold pasta and I'm going to go upstairs and have fun like a normal person." He turned around.

"Bitch," Linda muttered. She went upstairs and Mr. Sam followed her. They disappeared into their bedroom and it was quiet again.

I was hurt and offended. They didn't want me here. Well, I didn't want to be here. I didn't like Mr. Sam enough to compensate for this kind of condescending lecturing. I wanted to go home but it was a four-hour drive and they were leaving tomorrow evening either way. I thought about calling a taxi but decided to stay. I rolled onto the couch and turned on the television. However, the blaring TV was still not loud enough to silence the bedroom noise coming from upstairs.

Chapter 36

We gorge ourselves with vices
with food and money and women
By the time we meet our soulmate
we're already too late.
The world is over
and now I see you

Much after a very eventful life.

Can you forgive me?

I wish I had met you sooner.

The next morning I woke up to the sound of my cell phone ringing. It was Richard. I answered. "Hello?"

"Did I wake you?" he asked.

"Oh um, it's okay, I should be up anyway. Is everything okay?"

"I guess I was just checking up on you."

"It's not great but I guess that's okay. All they did was have sex the last two days. I thought I was going to get pregnant just from hearing them."

Richard laughed. "That bad, huh."

"Yeah. But I'm glad you called. I feel a little better about it now."

"Are you still jealous of Mr. Sam with other women?"

"Yeah, basically. I probably should get over it but it's tough letting go. You know. I can't seem to tell if love stays real even after it's over."

"Are you guys over?"

"Don't be too excited," I joked. "I still love him and I'm going to play his game for a little longer, I can't give up now. I've put way too much time and energy into this relationship. Nothing is going to make me leave now."

"Well said," he agreed.

"Were you really worried about me?"

"Yes, I was."

"That's so sweet of you. I appreciate that. What about you? Any bad dreams."

"Not last night. Which is unusual because Saturday nights always give me nightmares."

"I'm glad you didn't have one."

"Yeah, me too."

I said, "Are you still feeling sad?"

"Not right now," he replied honestly.

"Why do you think that is?"

"Maybe," he began slowly. "Because I'm talking to you."

"Oh you," I chuckled. "You don't have to humor me."

"No. Really," he said. "You make me happy. Please go on a date with me. I promise I won't let you down. It'll be fun. Magical even. You just have to trust me."

"Richard. I told you, I'm not comfortable with dating a patient."

"Well, what if I switch therapists? Then would you go out with me?"

Huh??? "No. I don't want you to leave. Just… give me some time. I'll think about the date thing. It's just I'm kind of worn out from being with Sam. He's kinda driving me crazy."

"All the more reason to date me," Richard complained quietly.

"I know. Just be patient. Please. I really need you to not interrupt this journey I'm on."

"You're on a journey?"

"Yes. Ever since I met Sam, I have been blown away by the world he has shown me. I don't know how to explain it. I feel like I've grown so much from the experience. Without him, I would just be…." I stopped myself, trying to think of how to finish my sentence.

"You'd be perfect," Richard completed for her.

I let out a breath of air. "I have to go now, Richard. Promise you'll call again. Any time you need anything I'll be there for you. Like you were there for me this weekend."

"Not a problem," he replied.

I hung up and spent the rest of the afternoon watching movies while the noise coming from upstairs stayed loud and consistent.

Ew

Chapter 37

Even when you're gone
I'm glad you left
Even when you're here
I wish you'd leave
I never meant to hurt you
I just thought you were full of shit.
My last pair of dice rolled a snake eyes
You weren't even happy for me when I left the table
because all my money was gone
and I had the strength to give up
Why are you never proud of me

So later that night, we packed our bags and climbed into Mr. Sam's convertible. He turned the music way up loud and I thought I would go deaf. However, the loud music did promise a peaceful ride home, protecting her from the girls and their snot attitudes. The only reason I even considered thinking I had a good time at the beach house was because of her conversations with Richard. He had been so understanding and considerate. It made her heart beat in her chest every time she thought about him. What was wrong with her? Could she be considering a relationship with a patient? It went completely outside of her work ethic. But shouldn't' love be the one reason to break a rule like that? And did she love Richard?? Even just a little?

What was she talking about? She didn't love Richard, she loved Mr. Sam. I was afraid I had disappointed him this weekend. The music kept everyone from talking which was a plus. It gave me time to think. I felt bad for ruining everyone's good time and decided if it was that big of a deal, they should probably stop inviting her to stuff.

The ride was long and miserable. I wondered if I should break up with Mr. Sam before it was too late and I embarrassed myself any further. Not to mention the fact that his other girlfriends obviously hated her. I was glad when we got back to my place.

"Can we come in," Mr. Sam asked.

"I have work in the morning," I replied lamely.

"No worries. Maybe another time."

"Okay," I agreed, maybe another time. I went inside and took a shower before going to bed, my head confused with thoughts of Mr. Sam and the weekend with him and the girls and the intimate phone conversation she had with Richard. The thoughts spun in her head and she fell asleep dizzy with stress.

The next morning, she waited eagerly for her appointment with Richard. She wanted to see him again and figure out her feelings from the conversations they had shared over the weekend. When Richard came into her office she felt self-conscious. Was she supposed to speak to him like he was a patient, or was this like a date?

"Good morning, doctor," he said.

She decided to treat him like a patient. It was safer for her that way. Safer for her heart. "So what would you like to talk about today?" she began after clearing her throat. "Are you still sad?"

"Oh, that." He shook his head. "Of course." He looked a little disappointed by the formality but I decided that I didn't care. "Yeah I've been feeling down but, you know, after talking to you over the phone. I have to admit I feel a little better."

"Yes, I was concerned about your reoccurring nightmare. You said the car flips over in a car accident. And you blame yourself because you had too many drinks."

"Yes," he agreed. "Something like that."

"What else can you tell me about your worries?"

"To be honest, my biggest fear," he replied, "Is falling in love."

"Why's that?"

"If I fall in love, I'm scared the story is over. What comes after that?"

I frowned. That was actually kind of a good point. "What does come after that?"

"I dunno. Babies maybe? I'm not sure. The end of a chase."

Chase? "So you don't want life to be over just because you fell in love."

"Yeah basically."

"Do you think that your fear of falling in love may be contributing to your depression?"

"I mean maybe. Maybe that is one of the reasons I'm sad. I don't know." He sighed. "The best part of my life right now is my job. It keeps me busy and I like what I do."

"Then do it," I insisted, "put all your focus into work. Make every last drop of doubt go into your job. It's important to stay busy when you're dealing with depression."

"You think so?" he asked

"I do."

He looked at me and smiled. "Why won't you go on a date with me?"

Great. This again. "I thought you were afraid of love."

"I am."

"I thought you said ending the chase would ruin your life."

"It will."

"Then why do you keep asking me out?" she asked exasperated.

"Because," he paused before continuing. "I think I love you."

I gaped at him in shock. "Excuse me?" she asked.

"Don't make me say it again."

"I can't do this right now Richard. I have a boyfriend."

"Yeah, and he's a polygamist. You could do better. I could be yours only. I could take care of you."

"Even if all that's true," I snapped, "I don't want to…"

"To what?" he asked.

"To…" He asked.

"Fall in love. Once I fall in love it's over. Like you said." I finished.

"What comes after the chase," he muttered.

"Richard."

"What? Your session is over. I have to meet with my next patient."

"Can I call you?"

"Yes, I'm free all day every day. Just call and we can talk more about anything you want."

"Okay."

Richard got up and left and I let my next patient into my office.

The chase. Love. Once you fall in love, is that really the end? She wasn't sure.

Chapter 38

I knew it was over
because I loved you
and I knew you'd never feel the same
because you promised me, forever.

Tae and I had been becoming better and better friends. I was glad when she called and asked if I'd like to go out for drinks. We met at the tavern the one I was a regular at and sat at the bar in my usual spot.

Dave came up to us and exclaimed. "You've brought a friend? Great. Where have you been the last few weeks? You haven't been around."

"Just busy. It's good to be back." I gestured to my friend. "This is Tae." I continued. "Tae, this is Dave."

"Nice to meet you," she said.

We ordered our drinks and I told Tae about Mr. Sam. "I was so embarrassed," I sighed.

"Why were you embarrassed?" she asked.

"I think the girls were mad at me because I didn't want to join their orgy."

"That's so lame."

"I know, right?"

"What did Sam say?"

"Sam said he invited me because he thought it would loosen me up."

"What the hell is that supposed to mean?"

"He wanted me to have sex with him and I didn't and now I think he's mad at me."

"I can't believe him," Tae replied. "He sounds like the worst person in the world. You should break up with him."

"I don't want to," I said. "I know I should but I love him and I want him to love me too."

“Then you’re just going to have to have sex with him.”

I frowned. “You think?”

“I mean that’s what you want too, don’t you?”

“I want to stay a virgin. I’m saving myself for marriage.”

Tae almost spits out her drink. She said. “I don’t think Sam sounds like the type to wait for marriage. The guy is scum. You need a respectable gentleman that is good to you.”

“Like a soulmate,” I agreed. “yeah maybe you’re right.”

“Think about breaking up with him.”

“I will. That does sound more realistic.” I downed a shot of whiskey. “He was so nice to me when we first met. Before he told me about his other girls. I was so happy when he noticed me. I thought I’d love him forever.”

“Forever is really long,” Tae replied.

“I know it is. And I don’t think it’s going to happen with him. Do you really think I should break up with him?”

“Yes,” Tae said. “I do.”

“I guess that’s something to think about.”

“Definitely.”

I asked her something very strange after that. “Do you think love is a bad thing?”

“I don’t think love is a bad thing. I think Sam is a bad thing. What about it?”

“One of my patients said something interesting to me?”

“What did he say?”

“He said once you fall in love the story is over. He said he didn’t know what came next. I thought he made kind of a good point.”

“How is that a good point? It’s depressing.”

“What does happen after you fall in love,” I asked her.

“Obviously. You get to be happy.”

“Happy?”

“Yes, you get to be happy forever. Love is a good thing.”

“I suppose.” I slugged back another shot. “Love is a good thing,” I murmured. “I know you’re right. I just have to figure out what I’m going to do about Sam.” you take my hand and I let you and you apologize for being so mean to me.

I forgive you and then we go back to never seeing each other again.

It was a couple of days later that I got home from work and Mr. Sam called. She wasn't sure what to expect from him. I knew I had been a loser at his beach house and she couldn't help but wonder if he was mad at her.

"It's very important, Christina," he said. "I have to see you?"

"Let me guess," I replied. "You want to come over?"

"Maybe, but that's not what I was thinking. Can I take you out for dinner tonight? I need to talk to you."

I wasn't sure how I felt about that so I agreed. After all, they were kind of dating and he sounded like it was urgent. "Now is this something personal or is this a need to talk to a professional therapist."

"Personal. A hundred percent." He finished. "I'll be there in an hour. Maybe sooner. I'll call."

"Okay. No problem," I said. We hung up the phone and I wondered to myself what the hell he was so excited about. Maybe he was going to break up with me? Was he that mad that I had rejected him all weekend? I didn't know but I guess it wouldn't be long before she found out. Sighing, I brushed my hair. I was still dressed in my slacks and cardigan I had worn to work. I didn't dress up beyond that because I was pretty sure we were breaking up. And if they were just going to break up, she wished he had just gotten it over with and told her over the phone instead of dragging it out like this.

My phone rang and he told me that he was pulled up front. I went outside and got into his car. "So what's this super important news, you wanted to tell me?" I asked.

"I don't feel comfortable saying it now. I'll tell you at the restaurant."

"Sure," I replied. We drove somewhere extra fancy and I thought to myself how stupid I looked. Would they even let her into the building? She was wearing loafers for crying out loud. "I'm not dressed up," I complained. "Why did you pick this place?"

"They know me," he said quickly. "Come on, let's go."

We headed inside and I was impressed by the size of the restaurant. The floor was marble, the ceiling was high and everyone was dressed elegantly. They set us at a table and Mr. Sam ordered us a bottle of wine.

"What's going on?" I asked again. "We're here. Tell me what you wanted to talk about."

"So the beach house weekend was a disaster. I think the girls were mad at you. Not only that but all they wanted to do was have sex. Sooo…"

“Sooo…?”

“So I dumped those sluts. I want to be exclusive with you. Just you and me. Like you thought when we met. No open relationship. No polygamy. Just us two.”

My jaw dropped. Really? So this relationship with him wasn’t the stupidest thing I had ever done in my entire life? Did I finally do something right? “Really?”

“Yes, really,” Sam said. “I really like you. And I want to see more of you. You mean a lot to me and I don’t want to lose you just because of a few bad girls.”

I was shocked. I couldn’t say no. This was really important to me. “Then my reply is yes. I’ll date you exclusively.” I felt my eyes tear up just a little. “That makes me really happy Sam.”

The wine came and we toasted, tapping glasses, to our new relationship. She was excited. This was what she had hoped for since the day she first met Mr. Sam at the bar she frequented. It was all so exciting she thought she was dreaming. But it wasn’t a dream. Mr. Sam was real in front of her and he wanted to be with her. She covered her mouth as he put a ring on the index finger of her right hand. “This is a promise to be just us two,” he said. “It’s not an engagement ring yet but give me some time and we’ll see what happens.”

Dinner came and I couldn’t even concentrate on the meal. I was ecstatic. I rarely ever got exactly what I wanted and I felt like this was it. Exactly what I wanted. Maybe I was becoming a better person from meeting Mr. Sam. Was he making me perceive things differently compared to before she had met him? She felt like a princess. When dinner was over, he drove me back to my place and asked if he could come inside.

I was scared and told him so. “I’m saving myself for marriage,” she admitted. “If I let you in, we might have sex and that would ruin this perfect night.”

She crushed her eyes shut, waiting for his rebuttal. Instead, he said gently, “I don’t want to ruin the night either. So don’t worry about letting me into your apartment. I’m tired anyway.”

She was shocked. He wasn’t going to press and beg to come inside until I gave up and let him in. Could it be that she wasn’t the only one growing from this relationship? Was he growing too? It all sounded too good to be true. “Good night,” he said.

"Good night."

I went back to my lavender apartment and threw myself onto the bed. Mr. Sam finally liked me. I was excited and scared at the same time. Why the sudden change of heart? Or worse yet, what if she was just dreaming? She pinched her wrist and it hurt. No. Not a dream but as good as one. I closed my eyes and instantly fell asleep.

I went to work the next day cheerful and playing with the ring on my finger. I wanted to relive the night before over and over again. I got to my office and was aghast to see Richard inside. She had completely forgotten that he was her first patient today.

"Doctor!" he called out loudly. "You're here. How are you?"

"I'm good," I choked. Shoot she had almost broken up with Mr. Sam and it was all this nitwit's fault.

"You look kinda," he made a circular motion with his hand, "Kinda pale. You okay?"

I cleared my throat. "What can I help you with today, Richard."

"So professional," he replied. "I thought we'd be a little more casual by now."

"Let's get this straight Richard," I said, almost angrily.

"You and I are not dating. You're my patient and I'm your doctor. Enough of this fantasizing about me. And I mean it."

He looked taken aback by what I had said. "Sorry. Just thought you looked upset is all."

"I'm not upset. I'm happy."

"Then why are you yelling at me?"

I said firmly. "I have a boyfriend."

"The polygamist right?"

"He's not a polygamist anymore. He picked me."

Richard gaped at her. "He did?"

"Yes and Sam and I love each other very much so please stop hitting on me, asking me out on dates, and telling me what to do. You have no right."

To my shock, Richard stood up abruptly. "I don't need this kind of shit in my life," he muttered angrily. "I gotta go." He stalked out of the room and left me by myself. Was it something I said? Just kidding. She knew she was being mean but he had to get it through his head that she was never leaving Sam for him.

I slammed my office door shut and dropped back into my black chair in front of my desk. "Ugh." I groaned. Just when things got good, it got equally bad. Her life was like a casino poker table and the best she could do was break even.

No worries. She wasn't going to let one patient ruin her day. She had plenty more work to do and if anything, this was a good thing. Richard was no one to me. Just a client. And he had no right trying to wreck her love life.

Chapter 39

You paid attention to me
You did everything to keep this relationship going
I wasn't sorry when we broke up
I'm no good at the dating thing

That evening, Tae came to my apartment for drinks. We sat on my couch and munched on strawberries with our wine. "I have some good news," I squealed.

"Oh no, don't tell me this is about Sam again."

"It is." I showed her the promise ring. "He asked me to date him exclusively."

"Really?" Tae said in shock. "There's something I never saw coming."

"I'm so happy."

"What about his girlfriends? What happened to them?"

"They're gone. He broke up with them. I couldn't believe it. I thought he was so into them."

"What can I say?" Tae shrugged. "Guess I was wrong about him. I'm glad you guys worked this out. I was so worried about you."

"I guess everything worked out perfectly," I murmured. "I think I love him."

They ran out of wine so I went to the cupboard and grabbed another bottle. I sat down again next to Tae. "I want him to love me too."

"Maybe he does."

"Maybe."

I pulled out my phone and scrolled down to a picture of me and Sam I had taken from my cell a couple of days earlier. "That's Sam."

"Wow," she exclaimed in disbelief, "he's gorgeous. No wonder you didn't want to let him go."

"Yeah, well, it took some getting used to."

"I bet." She paused. "Well, I personally don't trust him. I couldn't even imagine being with a guy like that. So you can keep him. I'm looking for something a bit more casual, someone that makes me feel safe and secure."

"I don't think I ever asked before," I said. "Do you have a boyfriend?"

"No. Not right now. I moved for my college and left behind my ex-boyfriend from high school."

"Oh, I see. Do you guys still talk?" I asked.

"Not really."

"When was the last time you talked to him?"

Tae pursed her lips together in thought. "About eight months ago. It's been a while."

"I see. You should get him to come up here," I encouraged her. "Then you two can go on a double date with me and Sam."

"That does sound fun. And he might even go along with it if he didn't replace me already."

"Why don't you call now?"

"I couldn't."

"Come on it'll be fun." I pushed jokingly.

"Okay fine." She pulled out her phone and dialed up her ex-boyfriend's phone through speed dial. He picked up and she exclaimed, "Josh it's been a while."

"Yeah, I know. What's up? You haven't called in a while."

"Well, me and my friend were just thinking something fun, not a huge deal but maybe we could all go out sometimes. She has a new boyfriend and she wants to go on a double date with you and me."

"Oh, that sounds fun. When would you want to do this?"

She put her hands up and shook her head at me. "What day?" she asked me, whispering.

"I don't know, this weekend maybe?"

"This weekend?" Tae repeated

"Sounds good. It's going to be a long drive for me, maybe like three hours so I'll try to get there as soon as possible. Saturday around noon?"

"That'd be great."

"Okay, see you then."

They hung up and Tae and I started giggling hysterically. I felt like I was in high school again with my best friend at the time. Back then, they would have so much fun doing the most mundane things. Now that she was older, she could appreciate how good her life had been then.

Chapter 40

I'm here now
is what we say when it's too late
I always wanted to meet you
I think it's special like that
when you get what you wanted so perfectly
and the dreams take over

Mr. Sam took me to a nightclub the next night. It was surprisingly busy for a weekday but it looked classy and fun. I wore a short strapless black dress and heels. I wasn't used to the excitement but I dressed nice and felt confident with Mr. Sam. We sat at the bar for drinks. Mr. Sam ordered us some shots before turning to look at me. "You look amazing," he exclaimed. "Thanks for coming out with me."

"Of course," I replied. "I love hanging out with you."

"I'll take that as a compliment." He said. "Do you mean that?"

"Every word of it."

He grabbed my hand. "Let's dance." He pulled me onto the floor and we began dancing to remixes of popular songs. I was enjoying myself. I couldn't believe how much fun I was having. Mr. Sam was everything I ever wanted in life. So much so that it was almost scary. I wanted to keep the memory of this night in my head forever. I wanted to relive this dream for all eternity. Just us two. On the dance floor. And I was happy. When Mr. Sam was around, I would get to be happy. It was as if he were the genie he joked about when they first met.

We danced to each song, one at a time. It took all my effort to keep from getting tired. My feet were starting to hurt so I got Mr. Sam's attention and told him I needed to use the restroom. I headed to the bathroom and washed my hands with soap and water. I checked my makeup and reapplied a layer of red lipstick. When I was done, I left the restroom and sat back down at the bar. She was worn out already and they had just gotten there.

Mr. Sam appeared behind me and kissed the back of my neck. "Hello miss. Is this seat taken?" he joked.

"Not at all, stranger," I joked in return laughing as he pulled her off the stool and lifted her up in his arms.

"Gotcha!" he yelled.

"Put me down," I laughed.

"If you insist, Miss Christina." Mr. Sam put her down and they ordered more drinks. We took our seats at the bar. He asked me. "You know, you should come live with me. Quit that job of yours. We can have fun all day long."

I was a little shocked and wasn't sure if I should be flattered or insulted. "You don't think I should work?" I asked, tipsy but confused.

"It's a waste of time. I can take care of you. You don't really need to work."

But I loved working. It was my life. I had worked so hard to get to where I am today. I couldn't possibly quit now. "Is this a joke?" I asked uncomfortably.

"No," he said. "I mean it. Come be with me."

"I have to keep my job," I said quietly. "I'm sorry if you thought otherwise."

He frowned and drank his drink. "Just thought I'd help you out. No biggie. No point in making a big deal out of it."

I felt bad for disappointing him but it was important for me and him to be on the same page about things like this.

"Why do you like that dusty old job anyway," he muttered. "How much fun can you possibly have talking to mental patients all day long? You're going to get a brain tumor."

"I'm not leaving my job, Sam," I said again.

"Fine." He shook his head. "It's not that big of a deal." He grabbed her arm and pulled her back out onto the dancefloor. They started dancing again and I decided to go back to enjoying the night.

Chapter 41

All I have left
Since you've been gone
Is my memory of you
And every time I ever made you smile

It was Saturday, and Tae and I would be going on our double dates. I'd be with Mr. Sam and she'd be with her ex from high school Danny. I was looking forward to the date. It sounded fun and I was curious to see how Sam would get along with my friends. We arrived at the restaurant at around seven and Sam and I found Tae and Danny already at a booth table.

"This is Danny," Tae said, gesturing toward her friend. "And you must be Sam?"

"Yes, that's right."

"And this is my friend, Christina. I'm Tae."

When we were all introduced to one another, we sat down with Tae and Danny and looked at our menus. We were at a restaurant called Giant Catch, a seafood restaurant I had been dying to try out ever since it opened up a year ago. "There's so much to choose from," I commented.

"Yeah," Tae said. "This place is great. I come here all the time."

"What's the best thing on the menu?" Sam asked. "I don't eat much fish."

"I like their fried shrimp basket," Tae replied.

"I might try that," he said.

"Oh they have flounder here," I exclaimed. "I've always wanted to try that."

The server came and they ordered their meals and drinks.

"So Danny," Sam began, "Are you in school?"

"I am."

"What are you studying?" I asked.

"Engineering," Dann replied. "And you?"

"Explorer," Sam declared.

I chuckled a little. Sam wasn't dropping the explorer thing. Maybe he really did consider that his job?

"What do you explore?"

"The world. I've been to every country twice. Spoken every language once. And I'm an all-around good-looking guy." He smiled and lifted a glass of wine before sipping from it.

"Huh," Danny said. "Sounds interesting."

"I even climbed to the top of Mount Everest. Ask Christina. She was there too."

"You both climbed to the top of Mount Everest?" Danny asked.

I replied. "He's kidding."

"Ha. you caught me," Sam laughed. "But I am an explorer. That part's true." He looked at Tae. "What's your poison? Where do you work?"

"I'm pre-med in college."

"What's your major?"

"Psychology."

"Oh like Christiana?"

"Basically," she replied.

The food arrived and we all began eating. I had to admit, my meal was delicious. I was glad to finally try the fish there. I wouldn't be surprised if I got fat in one night just from eating so much of their food. The servings were gigantic and I was hungry. I glanced over at Sam who was eating fried shrimp. He noticed me and asked, "How's your meal?"

"So good," I replied. "How's yours?"

"Good. Reminds me of when I was in Texas with a friend of mine. There was a restaurant called The Fish Market. They had good shrimp there too. The best I ever had, I think," he said.

Sam said. "Did you guys know Christina and I skydive together?"

"Really?" Danny asked. "Is this another joke?"

"No, we really do that," Christina said. "I was scared at first but it's actually kind of relaxing."

"It's freeing," Sam agreed. "It makes you feel like a bird flying in the air."

"I always wanted to go rock climbing," Danny said. "Never got the guts to do it though. I'm also kinda afraid of heights. Even so, I always thought it could break my phobia if I ever did it."

"That's so brave," Tae sighed. "I'm scared of everything. I can't even put my shoes on without checking to see if there's a spider in them. And as for heights, forget about it."

Danny laughed. "I remember the first time I saw her reaction to a spider in the car. She freaked out and I almost got into a car accident with her jumping around all over the place."

"And germs," Tae added. "Don't forget germs. I'm so scared of getting sick. It's my worst fear of all."

"Germs, huh," Sam commented. "And you're going to be a psychiatrist. That's kinda funny."

"Well, no one's perfect," she laughed.

"That's true."

Danny returned to the conversation about their skydiving. "How do you even go about becoming a skydiver?"

"You have to get a license," I replied.

"How do you get a license," he asked.

"You take classes, then you take a test, and then you have to pay for the license."

"How much does that cost?" he asked.

"About three thousand dollars each," Sam said. "I paid for it."

"Does your exploring job pay that well?"

"His parents are rich," I interjected. "He's a spoiled brat. I don't think he's worked a day in his life."

"Oooh okay, well, that's cool," Danny said. "That must be nice."

"Just lucky I guess."

Tae asked. " What job would you have done if you weren't rich?" Tae asked.

Sam was quiet, before replying, "A male stripper."

"I was being serious," Tae said.

"So am I."

"Isn't there any job you would do if you had to?" Tae asked.

"Well, maybe."

"What is it?"

"Farmer," he replied finally.

"Really?" I said. "I never would've guessed."

"Why farmer?" Tae asked.

"I like the idea of working for myself, making my own schedule, living off the land. I don't have to rely on anyone. You know, like with my parents. They give me whatever I ask for and I get a guilty conscious once in a while because I constantly rely on them for money."

"I can't even imagine." I said. "I've always worked for everything I had. My parents died when I was little so I had to work extra hard for everything I had. I bounced around from one foster home to another all the way up until I was eighteen. I had to get the biggest loan just to pay for college tuition."

"Oh, that's so sad," Tae said, putting a hand to her heart. "I'm so sorry honey."

"No problem. I survived and now I'm settled in my job and I have Sam." He took my hand and I let him. "I'm pretty happy now. I guess all that hard work paid off and now I get to enjoy life like everyone else."

"Cheers to that," Tae said, lifting a wine glass.

"Cheers!"

They toasted and I was happy.

Right?

Chapter 42

Do I know you?
Who are you?
Oh I remember
The one that broke my heart
How could I forget?

The next morning I went to work and found Richard in the waiting room. They had an appointment today. How could she forget? She let him into her office and shut the door.

"How are you today?" she asked.

"You know how I feel already," he muttered. "How's the boyfriend thing going?"

"Just fine, thank you very much," I said matter-of-factly.

"At this point, I'm surprised you're not already married."

"It's a little soon for that," I replied. "But he's nice to me and I like him."

"Nice," he complained. "I'm nice to you too. How come I don't get any credit."

"Are you drunk?"

"A tiny bit," he admitted.

"I thought we agreed you wouldn't drink as much anymore."

"I had one beer, five tops?"

"One or five." "Seven," he said. "I don't know. I wasn't counting."

"That's too much."

"Worry about yourself."

"I'm your doctor." "Then act like it," he snapped. "You obviously have a crush on me."

I was taken aback by his inane comment. "Excuse me," I said, voice raising. "You're the one that likes me. I'm just trying to help because you're my patient. What in the world gave you the idea I was in love with you."

"In love now? So you like me more than I thought."

"You're a jerk, you know that?"

"Sorry, I'm not perfect like your boyfriend. Skydiving and dinners and all that."

"You have a lot of nerve."

"And you don't have nearly enough. Just let him walk all over you. Like you're some kind of born victim. You don't take responsibility for your actions and you don't know something good even when he's throwing himself at you."

"Are you saying you're throwing yourself at me?"

"Yes, to put it bluntly. Yes."

"If you loved me you would go away peacefully and let me do my job."

"What's that supposed to mean?"

"You heard me."

"I just want to go on one date and you make it sound like I'm asking you to get cancer."

"You have too much free time on your hands." Why did it always have to be a big thing with Richard? He could have any girl he wanted and instead insisted on trying to make that girl be her. What was wrong with him?

"You're full of it," he said. "You know, when I met you, I thought this is a strong woman who knows what she wants and knows how to get it. Now that I've gotten to know you, I realize you have no idea what you're talking about. It's like you're backward. You date men who hate you, for one thing."

"Sam does not hate me. We're in love."

"Oh please. Don't give me that love crap." "If he didn't love me, why do you think he gave me this? She showed him her ring."

"He gave you a promise ring."

"Yes, he did."

"Well, whatever." He paused. "You know what, maybe he does love you. And maybe you love him, but you know what? I don't care. I don't care and I'm never going to." He stood up. "I'll be back for our next session. Let's try to keep it professional only next time. I can't take the stress this is having on my heart. You'll make me die young, at this rate."

I sat, completely flabbergasted. What in the world had I gotten myself into? I know what it looked like. It looked like I had gotten onto a way too personal level with Richard. But that hadn't been her intention. She wanted to be friends but was afraid of what that would mean. And Sam hadn't done anything other than be a perfect gentleman to her. Why did Richard have to hit her where it hurt?

I finished my day and started driving home. I passed a fast food restaurant and ordered a bacon cheeseburger with fries. I know I'm a vegetarian but I was so upset that I didn't feel like being me. When I had gotten my food, I bit into the burger and chewed slowly. She choked the entire thing down before reaching for her french fries.

When I was about twelve and staying with my current foster parents at the time, my foster parents started arguing while I was in my room. It was late at night and the screams and cruel words they threw at each other frightened me.

Fighting with Richard made me think of that time. Why was he so mad at her? And why did that bother her so much? Should she stop seeing him as a patient? If their sessions continued like this, she may not have any other choice. She sighed. What was she supposed to do?

She got back to her apartment and went inside. The lights were off in the apartment and it was getting dark outside. I sat on the couch in silence, trying to think of what to do. In life, we're faced with so many choices. I wouldn't mind so much except for the fact that I never seemed to make the right one. Her relationshipless life was now riddled with drama. She had always dreamed of a life like that. Now that she had it, she saw why most people didn't want it.

I fell asleep on the couch while watching TV. I couldn't stop thinking about Mr. Sam. He had been so good to her. He had put up with all her phobias and rejections and was honoring no sex till marriage boundary. They hadn't even kissed yet and he didn't seem to mind. Maybe Mr. Sam loved her for her. Maybe he was her soul mate. Like the fortune teller they had gone to see all those weeks ago, she had said she'd meet her twin star. Was her twin star Mr. Sam?

Veronica walked in and turned the light on. "Why so dark?" she asked.

"Sorry. Just thinking to myself." I yawned. "I think I fell asleep."

"Yes, you were sleeping."

"How was work?" I asked.

"It went well," she replied. "I had a good day. Hardly any problems. You look upset. What's wrong?"

"I got into a fight with one of my patients."

"That is very serious. What happened."

"I don't know if I should tell you."

Victoria joined her on the couch. “You can tell me. I keep good secrets.”

“Well, my patient has been asking me out every time he sees me. He wanted to go on a date and I told him I couldn’t because it was unprofessional. He’s my patient and I don’t date patients.”

“Why not? Is it Sam?”

“No. Yes. Maybe a little.”

“So leave Sam and date your patient.” “I don’t want to.”

“Then why do you talk about your patient so emotionally? Like he made you happy just from thinking.” I stared at Victoria. “Really?”

“Yes trust me. I know these things.”

“Sam and I are finally official and exclusive. I could never hurt him. He’s too good to me.”

“If you insist,” Victoria shrugged. She yawned and then went into her room and shut the door.

She wasn’t sure what to make of Victoria’s advice. Why wasn’t anyone ever rooting for her and Mr. Sam. Everywhere she went, someone was trying to talk her out of her relationship with Mr. Sam. Couldn’t they tell? They were two people in love and that was the most important thing of all.

Chapter 43

I spit beer on you
How was I supposed to know that the candy was poison
I spit beer on you
I hope it ruins your shirt.

I woke up the next day. It was Saturday so I didn't have to go to work. I wondered what Mr. Sam was doing and grabbed my phone. I dialed his number and it began to ring. For the first time in history, he didn't pick up. That was strange. Maybe he was out and had left his phone at home again.

I tried two more times but the phone went to voicemail.

I tried calling Tae to see if she wanted to hang out. No one picked up again. That was so weird. What was going on here? I hoped Tae was okay. I decided to see for herself. I dressed quickly in jeans and a gray hoodie and then headed out of her apartment. I got into my car. I had been to Tae's a couple of times now and I knew the address. It wasn't that long of a drive so she should be there in no time. She got to Tae's apartment door and knocked. There was no reply and instead, the door slowly opened just a crack. I pushed the door open the rest of the way and saw Tae and Mr. Sam on the couch having sex.

I thought I would pass out. Out of every nightmare I had ever had in my entire life this was the last thing I had ever expected to see. The two people she cared about the most and they had betrayed her.

They noticed her standing there and stopped.

"How could you guys do this to me?" I asked quietly. "I trusted you."

"Oh shoot," Tae said, pulling the blanket up to cover her nudity. "I'm sorry, Christina."

"Why?" Sam sighed wrapping a blanket around his waist and heading towards me. "I've been dating Tae ever since our double date with Danny. When we went to the restroom, we had sex. We've been together ever since."

"And you couldn't tell me?!" I snapped. "You tricked me. You kept this a secret from me. You're a terrible person."

"I was going to tell you later when I was ready."

"How could you do this to me?" I mumbled. "You gave me the ring. You said it was exclusive."

"I say a lot of things Christina. I told you that. I lie. And I never broke up with Bethany and Linda. I was just saying that so you'd open up a little. I just.... I just really wanted to have sex with you and you never do it, because of some weird promise to yourself that means nothing. And we all know the reason you're a virgin still is because no one wants you."

I started to cry. His words were vicious and cruel. I felt for the ring around my finger and took it off before throwing it at him. "I never want to see either of you two again. I hope you're happy."

I left the apartment, got into my car, and let my tears turn into a full-blown sobbing. I wasn't good enough for Mr. Sam. I should've seen that from the start. I wasn't good enough and now I was being punished. Her heart ached. And Tae had been such a wonderful friend. Tae had betrayed her too. How could she? I had to get out of there. As quickly as possible, she had to leave. She turned her car on and headed home.

When I got inside, my face was puffy and red from crying. Veronica rushed over to me, putting her hands to my face. "What's wrong, baby? Why do you cry so much?"

"Sam was cheating on me," I cried. "With Tae and Bethany and Linda and god knew who else."

"Sam again," Victoria said seriously. "I told you to stay away from. Didn't I?"

"You were right about everything. He's a liar. And a cheat."

"Oh, don't cry, don't cry." She reassured. "You're a big girl and there's no reason to cry. He's not worthy of it."

I nodded but cried harder. This was possibly the worst day of her entire life. What the hell had she been thinking? To think she had thought he changed. He was still a womanizing son of a bitch and she hated him forever.

Chapter 44

The birds chirped so loudly that day
It wasn't a bad thing necessarily
After all.
I needed the distraction.

That week, I went to work as if nothing had happened. I didn't pout, I didn't cry, and I didn't sulk. I just went through my patients and their problems as if I had none of my own. I don't know what gave me the strength to carry on. I didn't want anyone to know how hard I had been rejected.

When Richard came into my office for his session, I was almost happy. "Hello," he said. He was rightfully mad at her. "Richard," I began clearing my throat. "How are you doing?"

"I'm fine," he said. He stared at her. "Something's off about you today. Is something wrong? You look kind of pale."

"Oh. That. I guess I just didn't get enough sleep." Her vision was blurry as she scrolled down his notes and medications. "How's the medicine working out?"

"Fine." "Good."

"Christina, can I ask you something?"

"Yes, Richard, you can ask me?"

"Would you like to go on a date after work?"

She paused. "Yes," she said finally, "I'd love to."

He blinked. "Really? Are you sure?"

"I'm sure."

"What changed your mind."

"I don't know," I replied.

"What about Sam?" he asked.

"I broke up with Sam."

"I see," Richard said. "So you're single finally."

I nodded.

"What about all that patient, doctor no dating crap?" he asked.

"After the week I've had, I think I can make an exception."

He smiled at her. "Thank you." He paused before adding. "I'm so happy I don't really know what to say."

"Do you mean that?"

"Of course, why wouldn't I?"

I thought of Mr. Sam and all the lies he had fed me. Richard didn't seem to be that way at all. Had Richard been the one this whole time? She wasn't sure.

"It's nothing," I said. I took a deep breath. She was finally going on a date with someone who wouldn't hurt her. "So what are we doing tonight?"

"Do you have any requests?" he asked.

"Well, I did skip lunch. Could we maybe go out for something to eat?"

"Sure. Do you like seafood?"

"I do," I replied. "It's all I can eat that isn't vegetarian."

"I know a great seafood restaurant."

"Sounds fun."

"Do you want me to wait for you after work or pick you up at your place?"

"Pick me up at my place," I said. "I can text you my address."

"Then it's a date," he grinned.

This was probably the happiest she had ever seen him. And for that matter, the happiest she had ever seen herself. She hadn't expected that. She felt her heart jump as he spoke and thought to herself that she would be careful this time. She didn't want to end up getting hurt again.

After work, I headed back to my apartment. When I got there I jumped into the shower. When I was done, I fixed up my hair and put on powder, lipstick mascara, and a hint of blush. I dressed in a spaghetti-strap white dress and put on heels. She was determined to forget about Sam and Tae. This was her chance to be happy. She could feel it in her chest. Could Richard be the one to cure her loneliness?

Richard arrived about ten minutes after she was ready. She headed out to his car and climbed inside. He was dressed in a nice shirt and dress pants. He looked incredibly handsome and now that she wasn't rejecting him, he was starting to look pretty attractive to her.

"How was work?" he asked.

"It was good," I replied. "I love my job. I wouldn't have it any other way."

"I'm so proud of you," he said.

"Why's that?"

"I just feel like you've helped so many people. And even now, you're saving my life. I needed you and you appeared."

I thought about my break up with Sam and how desperate she had felt to replace the terrible memories with good ones and finally said, "I needed you too. I don't know what I would've done if you weren't here right now."

He turned some music on and she sat back in her seat. The music soothed her and she felt like it was medicine for her broken heart by Mr. Sam.

They got to the restaurant and went inside. It was a little ritzy and she wasn't sure who would be paying. She supposed it didn't matter either way. It wasn't like she didn't have the money. She was a working girl and working girls could take care of themselves.

They were seated at a table by a window. The lighting was perfect and there was a candle on each table. I ordered wine and Richard ordered a beer.

"I've never been here before?" I mused. "It's nice here."

"Wait till you try their lobster. You'll never go anywhere else again for seafood."

I agreed and when the server returned, we both ordered lobster and mashed potatoes. The server brought out a basket of bread and I took a piece and ate it. She turned her attention to Richard, wanting to know more about him. "So, you're an editor, aren't you?"

"Yes, for a fashion magazine."

"Do you like your job?"

"Oh yeah, I've been into fashion since I was a kid. I bought fashion magazines instead of comic books and my family thought for the longest time that I would grow up to be gay."

"Really?"

"Yeah, it was kind of a funny story. I went to prom with my girlfriend at the time and I think that was when they saw I was straight."

"So what can you tell me about fashion?"

"Oh, I get the greatest photographs to sort through. Each year is kind of like a magical theme that all artists abide by. What's in style depends so heavily on the customers so we find ourselves being torn between what's in and what's fresh and creative."

"That sounds amazing," I said, surprised by how much fun I was having. Richard was making the pain in her heart go away. Was that okay? Was she allowed to be that happy? Was this her second chance?

"Take a look at this," he said. He reached for a briefcase by his chair and opened it. He pulled out what looked to be a scrapbook. "These are my rough draft edits. This'll be a magazine in a couple of weeks and everyone will read it. The subscribers are the best part of my job. I love making them see and appreciate what I see when I think of fashion."

"Oh cool," I said, sincerely interested.

He showed me a couple more pages before closing the book and putting it back into his briefcase. "I'm going to pull an all-nighter. My deadline is tomorrow."

"Should we even be out if you need to work on your book?" I asked, feeling concerned. "I don't want to keep you from whatever you have to do."

"No worries. If it weren't for this date, I probably wouldn't even work on it at all and take the chance of being fired. Too sad, you know? But your company is giving me inspiration. We can stay here as long as you want. I promise it's not a problem."

"If you insist," she replied. She took a sip of wine. "You're just full of surprises, Richard. I want to buy the issue you're working on when it comes out. I may even subscribe."

"That'd be great."

"Well, you're a decent salesman."

He laughed and then I laughed too. Why had she avoided this for so long? Why had she ignored Richard every time he asked her out? If she had just picked Richard, she never would've had to go through what she did with Mr. Sam and his affairs.

"Do you believe in fate," I asked, unintentionally changing the subject.

"I do." "Do you think we're meant to be here right now? Together. Just like this. Do you think it's preordained destiny?"

He said. "I think it's meant to be, of course. Why do you ask?"

I sighed. "I just never believed in fate or destiny or even karma and God before. Being with you today has woken me up completely. I think I do believe in love. Like. I actually do. I believe in love."

"Do you love me?" he asked, looking at me seriously. "I do," I said, realization overcoming her. That's what all this turmoil was about. All this time she had spent trying to figure out who Richard was to her and now she knew. He was in fact, someone she loved very much. Forever even. "I think I love you," she said finally.

They leaned forward in their seats and kissed over the basket of bread. I pulled back in disbelief. My first kiss. It had been so natural. And I couldn't have imagined it being any more perfect than this.

The food arrived and we started to eat. The food was delicious. I felt my heart pounding in my chest. If this was just a dream, she didn't want to wake up.

"What changed your mind?" Richard asked. "What happened to your boyfriend?"

"He was cheating on me."

"Would you ever go back to him?"

"No," I replied. "Never."

"Would you like to be my girlfriend?" Richard asked, staring straight into my eyes.

All this time she had been searching for the right person to spend her life with. She knew now that the person she was meant to be with was Richard. "Yes," I replied.

And that was that. That was how I met my future husband.

Chapter 45

Your love has meant the world to me
I'm glad you're here
I've been alone my entire life.
Now I don't have to be.

I wanted to do right by Richard. There was a lot of emotional baggage I was carrying and I wanted to get it off my chest before Richard and I got too serious. I decided to put my skydiving license to use and use it one more time before I threw it out.

I thought about Sam and our time together and about Tae who I would always remember as a friend and lending ear. I wanted to forget and forgive them both. That was my peace of mind. I needed this. As much as I needed my job, and Richard, and my sanity.

I drove to the skydiving building and signed up for a jump. They checked my license and let me through. It wasn't long before I was on an airplane and had my parachute in the backpack on my back.

I was ready for anything and everything. When it was my turn to jump, I closed my eyes, outstretched my arms, and fell.

Being with Mr. Sam had been an adventure. Like the stories, he had told me of his travels and experiences. He was someone I would never forget for my entire life. He had been a lesson learned. With both pleasure and pain. I could never forget.

I spun my body and looked around me. The sky was a bright blue and the sun was shining. I pulled the cord to release my parachute. As I glided down, I thought about how much I had grown since meeting Mr. Sam. Even if we couldn't love each other. Even if they could never be together. I wanted Mr. Sam to know that from the depths of her heart, she forgave him. Even if they never saw each other again. She forgave Sam and Tae and Bethany and Linda forever.

She landed on the ground and lay down on her back. Tears came to her eyes and she was free. Free to be happy. Free to be loved. And with perfect trust and love came her feelings for Richard. He was her inspiration. Her hope. And she loved him. She thought about her first kiss with Richard and smiled even though she was crying. Everything was going to be just fine. She knew that now.

And the funny thing about it is, if I had to do it again, I wouldn't have had it any other way.